ONE MUST DIE

CANDICE PEDRAZA YAMNITZ
AMBER LAMBDA
SARAH EVEREST
CLAIRE KOHLER
LYDIA MAE
C.C. URIE

For permission requests, contact Candice Yamnitz at author@candiceyamnitz.us.

The story, all names, characters, and incidents portrayed in this production are fictitious. No identification with actual persons (living or deceased), places, buildings, and products is intended or should be inferred.

Cover and interior design by Candice Pedraza Yamnitz

Illustrations by Candice Pedraza Yamnitz First edition 2024 Names: Yamnitz, Candice Pedraza, author

Title: One Must Die/ Candice Pedraza Yamnitz, Amber Lambda, Sarah Everest, Claire Kohler, Lydia Mae, C.C. Urie

Description: Audience: Ages 13+. | Summary: Welcome to the annual game where teenage competitors search Sky Manor for the key to open a vault hidden behind the deceptive walls. The winner will have the wealth of a lifetime, but there is one catch. One contestant must die.

ISBN: 979-8-9881213-9-8 (paperback)

ISBN: 979-8-9881213-8-1 (e-book)

Subjects: Young Adult -- Fiction. | Mystery and Detective -- Fiction. | Teen & Young Adult Fantasy

"No one can serve two

masters, for either he

will hate the one and

love the other, or he will

be devoted to the one

and despise the other.

You cannot serve God

and money."

Matthew 6:24 (ESV)

You Are Invited

One must win and one must die

one key must be found

to unlock the treasures deep inside

friends and enemies must now collide

to fight for riches on the other side

keep your secrets close and your weapons closer

as you search the Sky Manor quicker than the other

sift through the truth and unravel the lies

remembering all the while

one must win and one must **die**

JESSIE SMITH
THE THIEF

ARDEN BENTLEY
THE BANKER'S SON

BENJAMIN NELSON
THE EMERALD PRINCE

CAMILLA CARRANZA
THE GOLD DIGGER

RUPERT NELSON
POOR SCOUNDREL

ZENITH LAURUS
THE OUTSIDER

MAPLE HILL
NICE GIRL

CHAPTER ONE

Jessie, the Thief

2:16 PM

WAKING UP ALIVE TOMORROW had the same odds as surviving a zeppelin crash. But that was the reality of this game—one competitor must die before someone would walk home with the grand prize.

I hunkered in my chair, empty suitcase between my boots in the zeppelin's cabin. Sweat soaked into my white shirt under my leather vest. The lacquered armrests reflected the mid-afternoon sun as the vessel shifted for the last approach to our destination. My fingernails bit into my palms, nerves needing something else to focus on than the eight of us competing in the game ahead.

Though a hundred invitations appeared like an apparition and dropped into our laps, most decided the risk of dying far outweighed the potential to win a lifetime of wealth. After all, one must die. They weren't the odds I would have hoped for, but the chance to win made the next eighteen hours worth the risk.

The hum of cogs and rushing air added to the tension between us riding in an oval cabin, facing each other in complete silence. I'd never been a word person. I much preferred equations and statistics. For instance, if all one-hundred of the people who received an invitation would have shown up, I would have had only a one percent chance of dying. Yet, in contrast, the probability of winning also skyrocketed with only eight players.

We lounged in our chairs, all separated by empty seats, the preparatory students on one side and the unfortunate souls with no scholarship or fortune on the other.

I tipped my hat lower over my eyes to hide the fear I might be exuding. No one glanced my direction. Instead, they held faraway stares as if they wrestled their own demons. My plan to win would be simple. I'd team up with the one person who might not want me dead.

Across from me sat the banker's son, Arden. Right now, he wouldn't dare give a nobody like me a look, with his fancy golden pocket watch tempting anyone to snatch it from him. I'd tried to speak to Arden before with all his prep school friends, but instead, I'd become a coward—the very thing I hated. My long-awaited message to him must be released from my chest. With such a big manor, I would get my chance to catch him alone easier. He glanced to his right.

The girl two chairs beside him had a nice-girl persona with a constant smile chiseled into her cheeks. She kept her luggage unattended on its own seat and a brown paper bag of who-knew-what on her lap, happily gawking out the window. She probably had a family that loved her, but probably also complained about how her rough-spun dress chafed against her skin. Her type inspired a gag.

Though she'd be a better companion than the couple several chairs to her right. The worst sort of people who thought of themselves as royalty. They cuddled together in their fancy clothes. The Emerald Prince with his blond hair and the condescending once-over he administered confirmed my nickname to be fitting. He ignored the gold digger clawing at his arm. She peeked out the window and scrunched her eyelids shut again, scared of the air below us. That's how you could be sure she was a gold digger and not one of them. The rich grew up taking zeppelins to their vacation islands that floated above the cities.

The poor scoundrel across from the couple had been an old chum once, Rupert. He wasn't the handsomest of the bunch, but his tan skin and jet-black hair added some allure. He flashed a daggered glance at the Emerald Prince, and I smiled a bit. Though that still wouldn't make us friends. Now, staring at his profile, I agreed with my previous decision about not keeping ties with people who flip like a coin in a dealer's hand.

The last two fellows didn't seem so bad. They chose seats on my side of the cabin like Poor Scoundrel (Rupert was too kind of a name for someone like him). The mousey man with a curly swirl of hair didn't have anything of use stuffed in any pocket that I could see. He gnawed on his bottom lip. Watching him had me sweating with nerves.

Then there was the outsider type. He kept to himself, in leather like me, and had nothing of value peeking from any of his pockets. But judging by his shifty eyes he carried something more valuable than jewels. If I made a guess, I'd say he dealt in secrets.

The outsider met my gaze. The hard set to his jaw and deadpan expression didn't invite further interaction.

The cabin jostled.

My hands gripped the armrest.

Movement stopped.

The windows on my side revealed a sixty-degree angle of sunlight hitting the clouds. On the banker's son's side, the view darkened to the shade of gray sandstone.

A young lady with wild brown curls, pilot goggles, and a leather coat with more pockets than I'd ever seen on one garment appeared at the front of the cabin. "We've arrived at Sky Manor." Her voice came out in a monotone cadence like she said this little speech often. "Arrive by 8:00 tomorrow morning. Those who are not at the port before departure will work at Sky Manor until the next game."

The declaration hit like an anvil on my chest. So this was why we were told to bring luggage for an eighteen-hour game where no one was going to think about changing into pajamas. Fear of dying had whipped up a thick dose of adrenaline in me, and now we also had to worry about getting stuck in a sky prison. I'd be eighteen in a year, five and a half percent of my life gone.

Her voice rang out like a gong. "All exit over here. Walk up the path into Sky Manor. Mister Woodhouse will give you further directions."

Emerald Prince toted both his and Gold Digger's suitcases as they lumbered through the open doorway.

"Shouldn't an automaton do this sort of labor?" the Emerald Prince asked.

"This is why I keep you around, dear." The Gold Digger smirked at him as she stepped around her boyfriend.

If any of us had to die or be left behind, I voted for the Gold Digger who clutched at Emerald Prince's occupied arm.

Even thinking those words made hives break out on my neck. The kids at the orphanage would be disappointed in me. I'd promised them that I would play nice. The reward for winning would feed all the children at my old orphanage and solve my own problems too.

The banker's son strode out, followed by Poor Scoundrel, Nice Girl, and lastly, The Outsider.

Why did I answer the invitation's call? Should I sit this one out by staying on the zeppelin? Not going would mean taking on bigger jobs and never being a legitimate member of society. I picked up my empty suitcase and sped through the aisle toward the exit.

The curly-haired fellow remained frozen in his seat. The news about being left behind must have frightened him enough to drop out of the game. A total coward who never would have won.

Good, more chances of me walking out with the prize. I continued past the pilot, catching metal wings with the initial "A" and the name Woodhouse etched onto her metal pin. *The surname seems to be popular up here.*

I stepped off the zeppelin and onto solid ground—well, as solid as a floating piece of land can be four-thousand feet in the air. Cool wind smacked me in the face and nearly took my breton cap with it. Light brown hair poked at my eyes, but I pushed it aside.

A long stone path lay ahead of me to an imposing building five stories high. The closer I got, the more I wondered about its history. In classes, teachers said that God yanked out the old abbeys from the ground to protect them from a warring populace, but the truth remained lost in time. Rows of trees cut into the shape of boxes encased the walkway in front of me. The contestants ahead turned a corner and disappeared from view. Though I didn't mind being alone, this place stirred unease in the pit of my stomach.

I rushed ahead.

My footfalls echoed.

The mostly empty luggage slipped from my sweaty palms and fell to the ground, flipping open. A few portraits and the old missive from my mom scattered atop the bare fabric lining, but that wasn't all. There was a foreign paper, folded and stamped with a wax seal, beside them.

Breath stalled in my throat. I kept my suitcase closed since leaving my rented room this afternoon. But there it was.

I picked up the yellowed missive and flipped it open:

The clock ticks on your watch.

The children play hopscotch.

The key can't save them all,

So be sure to attend the ball.

There is one closer than a friend,

Whom you must apprehend.

Chills spread across my flesh. Did they know about my sour dealing with the pawn shop over the silly watch? What did it mean by a person closer than a friend? I hadn't a real friend, only an orphanage of old women and children whom I'd visited ever since I'd aged out. Whoever wrote this couldn't know about my brother. I tucked the note in my pocket, gathered my luggage, and bounded up the path.

The pillared entrance doors remained wide open, and I ran into the building, unnerved by the strange poem.

An old man with wild white-and-gray hair flaring out from his head spoke to the others. I shuffled to a dark corner behind a pillar to overhear the rules.

"Remember, I am Mr. Woodhouse, the manor's mechanic and steward. I have the key to your bedroom doors and general maps of Sky Manor. You'll get a room for the night to stow your suitcase and sleep, should you choose. The rules are simple. Find the key and open the vault. The winner will get further instruction in the vault."

"Where is the vault?" Gold Digger asked.

"Ahhh, don't be so hasty. That's also part of the game."

"So." Gold Digger batted her lashes at Mr. Woodhouse with a ridiculous pose I assumed was meant to be charming, "what you're saying is that we can go anywhere in the manor to search for the key and vault?"

Emerald Prince removed his top hat, revealing a head of blond hair. He remained the gold digger's shadow, listening over her shoulder, positioning himself like a protective boyfriend. But I could read the hunger in his piercing green eyes. He wanted the prize almost more than his pretentious girlfriend did.

"Well, you can't go in the rooms of other contestants, but otherwise, yes." Mr. Woodhouse massaged at his wrinkled jowls without dropping his silly grin. "When you hear the bells—"

"Can we choose any room we'd like?" Gold Digger interrupted.

I tossed my gaze to the copper pipes on the ceiling. These two had my patience stretched to its breaking point already.

Mr. Woodhouse chuckled. "Yes, but—"

"Give me a key and a map to find my room. I want to start searching." The snide tone in Gold Digger's voice could kill. She ripped a key and map from the older man and signaled for Emerald Prince to follow suit.

Poor Mr. Woodhouse stood, mouth so wide he was ready to swallow a passing gnat. "But the bells call for mealtime in the dining hall. And for you each to attend The Cogs and Corsets Ball. Check the schedule on your invitations."

Gold Digger and Emerald Prince continued to stride away.

The banker's son took a key and paper. "Will you be giving any suggestions about how to win the egg? You know, the key to the vault?"

Mr. Woodhouse shook his head. "Not until the meet and greet in an hour. You've got to stick to the schedule or the manor will not release any more keys. The manor is not going to like this one bit."

The banker's son tipped his head, a signal of farewell, and marched off, indifferent to the rest of us.

I inhaled a steadying breath. This might be my moment.

"But I had several more passages in my speech," Mr. Woodhouse called after the fleeing contestants. The disappointment in his drooping expression kept me bolted in place.

Poor Scoundrel got his key and followed the others. The Outsider did the same.

Nice Girl called after the escaping contestants, "I brought a sweet treat for everyone."

"Oh?" Mr. Woodhouse drew nearer to the girl. "What did you bring?"

"A screaming peach."

His wrinkles contorted, bushy eyebrows furrowing.

"No," she giggled, "I mean they're peach scones from the Screaming Peach Café, my best recipe."

"Then, I will have one." He plucked a pastry. "We haven't a need for outside food here, so I haven't tasted anything from the city in decades. Our food just appears. All the automatons prepare and serve it."

Nice Girl watched him with far too much interest. Did she put poison in the food?

The old man chewed and nodded. "Here's the key to your room and the map. I was going to tell the others to be careful about following hidden doorways. That's how I got trapped up here forty years ago."

Eyes snapping wide open, Nice Girl trembled, making her bag jiggle. "Are you trapped in Sky Manor now?"

"No, no, nothing like that. Someone must fix the automatons." He slapped the brass back of a passing humanoid.

The robotic voice chirped. "Is there something you require, Mr. Woodhouse?"

"No, nothing, A57." Mr. Woodhouse rubbed his palms together and adjusted his brown coat with bulging pockets full of clues for me to swipe. He headed toward me. "Your key, my dear." He held out a brass key with the number 301 carved into a decorative cog at the top.

I snatched the cool metal and stuffed it into a pocket.

"If you need anything, I work below." He shifted on his feet and sped off.

Winning this game wouldn't be so easy with the other six ready to start a fight should they find any key. Well, Gold Digger might be the easiest to subdue.

My search began with me heading to the right. If the strange missive suggested a ball, I should find myself a gown, and I presumed Gold Digger wouldn't leave home without one or ten. My thieving skills would serve me well.

"Jessie," a young man said my name.

Though the person was familiar, I hoped he would ignore me. Even here, I couldn't get away from my own stupid mistakes.

Mister Woodhouse's Notes

Jessie—Main atrium—1 key
Strategy: Paying a ransom?

Arden—Second floor passage—1 key
Strategy: Giving off intelligent airs—not yet using them

Benjamin—Main atrium—1 key
Strategy: Taking his time because he seems to think he's the only one with any chance of winning

Camilla—West stairwell—1 key
Strategy: Alliance with boyfriend

Rupert—Broom closet—1 key
Strategy: Checking for a hidden door

Maple—her room—1 key
Strategy: Proffering scones - mostly rejected - Personal note: best scone I've ever tasted

Zenith—Kitchen—2 keys
Strategy: Setting everyone on edge

Vault-Hidden

CHAPTER TWO

Arden, the Banker's Son

3:34 PM

I'D ALWAYS ENJOYED COLLECTING secrets—I knew most of the other contestants' in this game, after all. But none of them knew I had both the highest and lowest stakes for winning life-changing riches. The secret of my own?

I was already dying.

And this could be my way out of my father's influence before I lost the chance.

I strode across the parlor, a side eye on my competitors as I scanned the room. How fitting to be in the game with *these* competitors, tangible reminders of just what I was fighting for. Tension from many of our "business" connections and generally unscrupulous motives had created quite the interesting zeppelin ride. In the first hour, I'd begun to think none of us would progress toward finding the vault, more afraid of letting each other out of sight or giving away personal strategies than of missing out on the purpose of this entire ordeal. Eighteen hours would go by as both a blink and a torture in this place; we'd be strategically tiptoeing on eggshells while simultaneously *trying* to stomp one another out. Thankfully, if there was one helpful thing I'd learned from my father, it was how to balance both of those things expertly. My strategy for the game would simply be what I'd learned worked everywhere else. A heavy dose of apathy and false politeness. I would search for the keys with wit and a level head while others were destroyed by their own emotions. I already knew the majority of the other contestants were run by them. I wouldn't fall into the same trap.

As I passed through a hallway toward a small set of stairs, Benjamin's pompous posture rounded the next corner, his modern style of fine fabrics sticking out against the mixture of antique pipes and wallpaper. *Speaking of someone whose emotions are easy to prod.*

I cleared my throat and continued walking on. In my peripheral vision, I could tell Benjamin turned toward me, but I ascended the stairway to his right, not giving him a glance. I was counting on it to really push his pretentious buttons since he was surely dying to confront me about the proposition I'd sent two days before the invitations had arrived.

Now I couldn't believe I'd stooped so low as to include him in my planning. It was simply a backup plan, and I had no doubts of my ability to reach my goals in this competition. But for now, I'd leave Benjamin with that delightful weight on his shoulders.

I marched up the small set of stairs straight ahead as Benjamin and Camilla veered to the side. Gaudy paintings and gold-gilded decor lined the sitting room—a room meant to entertain, complete with hot teas and lavish sweets laid out for guests to enjoy as they envied the grandeur of the mansion, but there was no actual living presence in sight. No different than the isolating way people like myself displayed wealth and status in the world below.

My throat dry, I was almost tempted to drink the potentially poisoned tea. I'd only heard rumors of this mansion before the invitation had arrived by literally falling into my hand from thin air. I'd always thought it to be a hoax, a silly fantasy to imagine a magical world of mystery in the sky above me—that something bigger existed outside my box of life where I was assumed to own the world because of my wealth. Funny how I'd turned out to be right. Other than the zeppelin ride through the clouds, nothing fantastical or awe-inspiring about this competition stood out. It held the same cutthroat race of life, only higher up so that those who didn't make it would fall harder and farther than ever. I wasn't surprised . . . and yet I realized how disappointed I truly was to be right.

I took in the carved clockwork of the marble ceiling, frozen and unticking. Something about the room unsettled me despite its familiarity to my world. As if it held a secret just out of sight, beckoning me to find it and prove there was something else to all the pretense. Perhaps it could just be that part of me still looking for something more. But that was something I wouldn't find until I won this game. So, I may as well chase my love of solving puzzles and mysteries to the end.

Hands behind my back, my gaze traced along the patterned wall to every section between the curtained panels and to a wall with a collage of small portraits containing no-name people who must be important to someone. *Are they the ones who won fortunes before? Or the unfortunates who died in the process, memorialized only on the walls of their death place?* A shiver crept up my spine and across my shoulders.

A gentleman dressed in a pilot's uniform looked back at me from his frame with alluring, weathered eyes, as if he had a great wisdom to tell. Likely something sappy along the lines of, "Don't be fooled. Riches and rewards can't buy it all." But for my sake, I hoped he was wrong, at least in this dire instance.

Searching for a crevice, a hidden button, anything that had the potential of revealing the secret key, I ran my finger along the pristinely dusted tops of the frames. I stepped back and frowned, looking at the pilot again, this time noticing the way those weathered green eyes matched a plant in the corner behind him. *Was that there before…?* The snake vine grew up and out of sight, past the frame. My eyes traveled up with it to the next frame above, where a subsequent vine protruded out of the bottom and to the left, where yet another continued strand began in the portrait beside it. The maze of ivy took me through each of the two dozen or so frames, ending at one in the bottom right corner, with no plants visible. *Interesting.*

I bent to inspect this final portrait, of a young woman with nothing of particular interest about her. But the background caught my attention again. A tiny sprout weaseled into the frame now, growing before my eyes. *How in the world?* I held the frame at the edges and lifted it gently off the wall. Nothing but the rose-printed wall behind it. Running my hand along the back of the portrait, nothing gave the trick away. I flipped it over to study the image further. The vine had bloomed, growing ever longer toward the front. Toward me.

It burst through the portrait, and I staggered backward to the floor, shielding myself.

Silence followed, no shards ever falling. Taking a deep breath, I wiped off my glasses before picking the frames back up. The young woman now held a red flower, a smirk on her face probably resembling the one I'd given Benjamin moments ago. Each of the portraits' eternally captured smiles seemed to snicker at me now, as if taunting me with my presumptions of this mansion being nothing extraordinary.

I released a mix between a chuckle and a snort, glancing around the room to ensure no one else saw the entire spectacle of foolishly falling over. The chamber was empty aside from myself. I tipped my head to the ceiling and blew out a breath of air.

What's that? I squinted. That was not there before. A carved vine creeped its way through the ceiling's frozen cogs, zig-zagging in and out like the pattern I'd followed through the portraits. It made its way through the entrance of the room and down the hall. I jumped to my feet and chased after the vine, my feet tapping as quickly as my pulse, alive with discovering a whimsical secret. Until the new ceiling decor veered into a fork and disappeared in three directions. One pointed down the staircase to the first room we arrived in, which we'd all combed over enough to divulge anything that would have been there. The vine crawled to the left and disappeared into a door down the hall. I edged toward the open room.

A library stretched before me with books and cozy footed couches set up in different sections. Someone else stood in the atmospheric lamplight, obviously a competitor and not one of the "maids," by the way she delicately thumbed through a book and placed it back on the shelf. But I'd recognize her anyway by her reddish-blond hair and nonchalant demeanor, sweet as the treats she often carried—starkly different from the rest of the people here. Not that I knew Maple anymore. I hadn't seen her since our chemistry class when I'd allowed myself to get a little too close. A mistake I couldn't make again. Not yet.

Maple glanced in my direction. My heart jolted at the way her soft brown eyes lit up. "Arden?"

I pivoted, briskly moving in the direction the vines led.

"Arden!" Her disappointed voice faded, not appearing to follow me in my mad escape.

There was no way the clue pointed to her. I'd never thought she belonged at that cutthroat school, and she didn't belong here either. I didn't deserve to speak to her. And even if I did . . . my father would retaliate without a second thought if I gave a mere scholarship acquaintance any lick of acknowledgement or power over me. A prominent banker's son couldn't bend to fraternize with those beneath his level. Leaving me with Father as my only true company, controlling my every relationship. The naive, younger me had clung desperately to the rumors of potentially having a half-sibling—a sister, the more specific rumors would say. Imagining our meeting was the only thing that got me through some days. But those days were long gone with the rest of my gullible hopes. Now, the only thing that got me through life was the idea of pushing my father out of the picture for good—so I could experience good for the first time. That was why I had to push my feelings aside for the duration of this game, no matter what came up.

Chasing the corridor to a light at the end, I nearly bumped face-first into an automaton servant. Its metallic face displayed only apathy, its inhuman eyes boring lifelessly into mine, but it gave me a short bow of its head before shuffling past me on its mission, carrying a wilted, potted plant.

Prickles climbed up my arms and legs, like every time I encountered the robotic attempts at recreating humanity. Partly because anyone would be unnerved by them. And partly because . . . I knew it was exactly what my dear father would gladly turn me into if the doctors could "save" me. As long as he could keep me around to do his bidding and grow his fortune. Whatever it took to keep our prestigious bank flowing with riches—to control me as a pawn for his legacy.

Just as he already is, isn't he? It was all I'd ever been. A living, breathing automaton with the ability to twist my face and my words as best served the business.

It was why I had no choice but to win this thing. If I could fall into riches beyond what my brain could even comprehend, then surely it would satisfy my father if I gave him most of it, paying out my share of the family business. My only peaceful chance to escape from under my father's grimy thumb—free from the darkened stains of spilled blood and thieving behind the pristine mask I'd been taught to wear.

If I could pull this off, though, I could truly live for the first time in my life for the couple years or so I may have left with this invisible sickness.

I could be a real person.

Pick up a hobby outside of writing threats.

Find someone to truly care about, who wasn't just another pawn planted in my circle.

I wasn't naive enough to think I could make up for the things I'd done in the name of business . . . but I could learn to do better moving forward.

After whatever it might take to get there.

The light-ended corridor led me straight into an enclosed conservatory. Familiar and strange plants alike flourished in garden beds and pots. Some glowed from the sunlight seeping in through the circular windows cut into the arched ceiling, but others appeared to give off glows of their own. Fog from the cloud layer just outside rolled into the edges and corners of the room, creating a mystical effect that may be unsettling to some, but I found oddly soothing.

I'd never been much of a plant enthusiast, but this surely must be where the vine hinted me to go. With plenty of ground to cover, I kneeled on the cobblestone floor that swirled with a layer of fog and dug my hands into the cool soil of the closest bed, searching for the metallic texture of a key.

"Never thought I'd see you getting your hands dirty." A deep male voice from the fog made me jump. Leaning against the corner nearest me, Zenith's piercing eyes glowed like the plants.

"You of all people should know my hands are plenty dirty." I put on my business smile, despite how slimy it felt. "Let me guess. You have something concerning Father's newest scheme, even while up here?"

"Something like that."

I clenched my teeth, not realizing Father actually had something going on with the competition. *Did he somehow get me invited himself? Surely even he doesn't have that power.* This was meant to be my one chance to make something on my own. I opened my mouth to inquire further about Zenith's comment, but he'd vanished. His boots silent against the stone, as befitting of an assassin and blackmailer, he must have slipped through the shadows of the corridor I'd come from. My spine tingled. I wouldn't admit it to anyone else, of course, but close family "friend" or not, I was almost as wary around him as with the automatons.

Calming down, I continued my digging through the pot in front of me, its flowers only beginning to bloom. I did a double-take at one, its petals different from what I remembered when I'd first knelt here, a stark white now tucked into the soft midnight blue bud. I took hold of the new, white petal with my index finger and thumb. A piece of paper.

I frowned and glanced back at where Zenith had been. He couldn't have placed it there without me seeing, not in our short interaction. *Could he have?* Unfolding the paper, a few wilted petals tumbled out like confetti. As I skimmed the few scrawled words, my fingers trembled.

"The test of a banker's true greed: claim the win or save your sister's life?"

Mister Woodhouse's Notes

Jessie—3rd floor—2 keys
Strategy: She's hunting for someone. Possibly wants an alliance.

Arden—Second floor passage—1 key
Strategy: Playing with the manor

Benjamin—Parlor—1 key
Strategy: Outsmarting everyone

Camilla—West stairwell—4 keys
Strategy: Keeping track of her boyfriend

Rupert—His bedroom—1 key
Strategy: Ransacking the room

Maple—Library—2 keys
Strategy: Exploring, making herself appear unthreatening

Zenith—Conservatory—6 keys
Strategy: Being everywhere all at once

Vault-Hidden

CHAPTER THREE

Ben, The Emerald Prince

EXACTLY 4:15 PM

SECOND CLASS.

Idiotic.

Ungrateful.

They were all words I would use to describe Arden Bentley.

I hated everything from his glasses to his thin frame. He was weak and unfit for the position his father was practically handing him. I knew he noticed me right away, even though he hadn't reacted to my presence. He was weak, and I was going to take advantage of it.

The mandatory meet and greet had started fifteen minutes ago and everyone was doing their own thing. Several people milled around, looking at the decorations in the parlor. Others talked in hushed voices. Camilla kept glancing at my loser cousin periodically through her scrutiny of the room. Arden followed her movements, as did some mousy girl who kept glaring at Camilla when she wasn't watching Arden. I didn't know what was going on between the two women, and honestly, I didn't care. I wasn't going to get involved in whatever childish spat was going on between them. Camilla had a habit of being at the center of drama, and I wasn't going to fan the flame during the competition.

Knocking back the rest of my drink, I set it on the automaton's outstretched tray. The robotic voice clicked and whirled as it offered to refill it. I paid it no heed as I turned my back on the machine. Not only did it *not* know how to make a proper drink, but I also didn't trust it. There was just something about the mechs that unnerved me. I wasn't sure if it was the lifeless eyes, the cold brass, or the lack of a feminine figure, but they weren't for me.

I came back to the conversation that I'd been zoning out of only to catch the man's hurried, "—quite interesting to say the least. I had the most trouble with the syncing mechanisms. You'll see at dinner. Two of the autos are about half a second late."

Nodding, I searched my mind for an excuse. The butler had introduced himself as Woodhouse—or something—and explained he was head butler and lead mechanical scientist. Why he needed to specify when he was the only living man here, I had no idea. But it didn't stop him. Everything about the man seemed a little *too* charged—like he'd been on the receiving end of an electrical current more than once. His wide, brown eyes never wavered from my face and he spoke with an intensity that would make anyone squirm.

The worst part? He'd been talking to me, and only me, since this silly meet and greet started.

His butler's attire was made up of a brown leather trench coat that hung all the way to his ankles. On it were enough pockets and buckles to hold an entire household's worth of coins and nick-knacks. I didn't know what was in them, but when I realized more than one of them were moving, I didn't want to.

Just then, a different movement caught my eye and I followed it. Arden was walking out of the parlor. The heavy weight in my pocket told me to follow him.

"But, of course, that reminds me of the—"

"That's extremely *fascinating*, Woodrow."

"*Woodhouse*," he quietly corrected.

Ignoring the comment, I continued, "But I really must find a washroom."

"Oh, it's out the blue door and down the hall to the—"

I didn't let him finish, my goal already in mind. I could feel Camilla watching me, but I didn't care. It wasn't any of her business anyway.

Arden left the door cracked so I could easily slip through after him. I tried to ignore the hall around me, but it was like nothing I'd ever seen before. Brass pipes crept up the wall like ivy, letting out little puffs of steam at the joints. Behind them I could make out pale pink wallpaper. I couldn't explain it, but it felt like the wallpaper had eyes. This place was as unnerving as it was fantastical.

Different types of potted plants sat six feet apart, decorating the hall alongside the pipes. Arden disappeared around an overly large fern and I rushed forward. The closer to him I got, the more exposed I felt. I didn't know if there were cameras set up in this house, and I didn't want to. Nor was I about to warn the others. I would just have to be careful about what I said and did.

Two seconds later, I caught Arden. He squinted at a painting as he cleaned off his glasses. Even alone he was pretentious. I cleared my throat and he jumped. Arden quickly slid his glasses back on and faced me. He looked me over for only a moment before a smug smile spread out across his face.

"Good afternoon, Mr. Nelson."

"I know it was you."

Arden's jaw ticked just once. "What was me?"

The weight of my pocket doubled and I almost reached for the note inside. I refused to give him the satisfaction of knowing

I kept it close. I took a few steps closer so he could just hear me say, "I know it was you who sent the note. Did you think I wouldn't figure it out?"

"Did you think I wouldn't figure out the state of your finances?" he challenged.

"So you admit it."

"What's the point in hiding it? If I didn't want you to figure it out, I would have been more careful, Benjamin."

I balled my fist, heat dancing at my fingertips. It would be so easy to end his life. The poison brewing and fermenting under my skin would kill him before he finished taking his first breath. All I would need to do is take my glove off and touch him.

"I can see that makes you unhappy," Arden said, pulling me from my murderous daydreams, "but I've been unhappy lately, too. Me and my father. I vouched for you, and you lost all that money."

"I can get—"

"You can *win* it back, you mean?" Arden's smug smile only twisted further. "I'm sure you were able to deduce from the note that I know exactly where that money went."

"So, what now?" I seethed. "If my father heard about this—"

"It was my father who informed me that yours cut you off. You're broke; that's why you came to me for a loan."

I wished I could say his words didn't find their marks, but they did. I was reminded daily of how I failed my father—of how I failed myself. I was in too deep, and Arden was supposed to be my way out. It was true, my father had cut me off, but he would see sense again. At least, he would if Arden hadn't threatened me.

"I can get you the money. I've always paid my debts."

"Your father has always paid your debts, Benjamin. And at this point, we're just speaking in circles. My note mentioned what I wanted. Now it's time to pay up."

My poison burned hot. Even though I thought Arden was stupid, he never did anything without a reason. It wasn't likely he would share his reasons with me, but now was as good a time as any to figure out what he wanted.

"Your note only said that you needed me. You never specified what."

"You aren't the only one who has a strained relationship with their father. And that's exactly what I need you for."

Realization dawned on me with a sickening clarity. Dread clutched me with its oily grip and squeezed. "I will not—"

"I don't think you appreciate the situation you're in, Benjamin. You do this for me, or I tell the headmaster you can no longer afford admission, your bookie where to find you, your associates to pull all their business, and even your trollop what a lousy gambler you are. *Do we understand each other?*"

Focusing on the feeling of the silk lining of my white kidskin gloves, I reminded myself they were still on my hands. I was a lot of things, but a murderer wasn't one of them. At least—not yet anyway. Every word Arden spoke, it brought me that much closer to taking my gloves off. My fingertips burned black, and

I knew the poison that waited there would be like nothing I've ever seen before.

"I do not have all day, Mr. Nelson," Arden said, faux respect shining through his words. "Do we have a deal or not?"

I couldn't move. Fury warred with hatred inside me—for both Arden and myself. This was my fault, and I knew it. I never should have placed that first bid. I've been running from my debts ever since. It's why I needed to win. I needed to clear my name and, in doing so, get both Arden and his father out of my life. But killing him...? I didn't know if that was something I could do.

"Perhaps you need me to sweeten the deal? Hmm?" Arden removed his glasses and wiped them again, as if we were talking about floral patterns instead of murder. "I would be willing to forgive up to half of the bank's debts."

Keep my social standing.

Debts forgiven.

One dead body.

As much as I hated to admit it, this was a good backup plan. One accidental touch and it would all be over. I went back and forth on it for a good while. Arden replaced his glasses and waited expectantly. An agreement was on the tip of my tongue, but I asked instead, "How long do I have to decide?"

"Until the treasure is found."

That meant there was still a good chance that I could get out of this on my own. I could win, find a nice girl who would actually support my choices, and leave this whole mess behind me.

I nodded, and Arden smiled. He then had the nerve to come up and clap me on the shoulder as if I was some business associate before moving on down the hall. I didn't follow him—I couldn't. The stupid keys and riddles could wait an hour or two. I needed to clear my head.

Rushing back the way I'd come, I rounded the corner. I collided bodily with Camilla, who stared up at me with wide eyes. Their brown depths were as familiar to me as the curve of her waist. Out of habit, my grip tightened on her. I couldn't go long without touching her. There had to be others like Camilla, but until I found them, she was the only one I could find comfort in.

It had been surprising to see her at takeoff. I hadn't told her I was coming, and she had never mentioned getting an invitation. The dress that hugged her figure was one I didn't recognize, and honestly, I didn't know where she'd gotten the money for it. It wasn't one I commissioned for her. Then again, I've been spending less and less on her lately. For one, I was no longer spoiling her—which she liked to remind me of—and second, she was going to be leaving soon.

It wasn't the right moment yet, but soon I was going to reveal to her that I knew her eyes had been wandering. I didn't care, I was using her too. But she wasn't getting what she thought she deserved out of this relationship, and the more she pulled away, the less I was getting out of it too. It benefited me that I was able to touch her bare skin without poisoning her. However, that meant nothing if she wasn't going to devote herself to me.

Despite all of that, I still pulled her in close. I kissed her neck and breathed in the familiar scent of her brown curls. I needed to lean on her for a bit—even if I wasn't going to tell her why. She already knew about my gambling problem and my poisoning ability, and that was more than I wanted anyone to know. I kept close attention to her hands and pulled back as one drifted down to my pocket.

Her brown eyes narrowed in irritation. I immediately went on the defensive, but knew what was coming all the same. She wanted to know where I'd been, but where I'd been was the last thing I wanted to talk to her about. I wracked my mind to try and find a way to manipulate the fight in my favor. The only thing I could think of was my poor cousin. I knew she still wanted him, even though it was me she chose to follow into dimly-lit cloak rooms and secret, high-end parties. She was becoming more and more of a distraction. Camilla was taking me away from my responsibilities, trying to spend money I didn't have, and was now messing around with my cousin on the side. My resolve hardened as I realized that maybe I would have to end things with her sooner than I thought.

Mister Woodhouse's Notes

Jessie—*East wing second floor—2 keys*
Strategy: Searching for alliance

Arden—*Second floor passage—1 key*
Strategy: Blackmail cliché

Benjamin—*First floor hallway—1 key*
Strategy: Not letting girlfriend have her way

Camilla—*West stairwell—6 keys*
Strategy: Highly attached to boyfriend

Rupert—*Dining room—1 key*
Strategy: Inspecting table too closely

Maple—*Dining room—2 keys*
Strategy: Trying to befriend Rupert

Zenith—*Hall cupboard—8 keys*
Strategy: Discovering all the manor's secret passages

Vault-*Hidden*

CHAPTER FOUR

Camilla, the Gold Digger

5:02 PM

"BENNY, HONEY, WHERE HAVE you been?" I slid an icy smile in place. A part of me enjoyed the way he clenched his jaw at the pet name. He'd never guess that he was my strategy, my ticket to winning before I cut him from my life.

"Are you trying to start a fight?" He clenched his fists. His nose flared, and he seemed in a daze.

Has he been drinking? The hideous pink walls with disgusting pipes jutting from their surfaces spun around me as if this hovering rock planned to tip us off course and drop us to our doom. Not just one would die, but the whole blazing lot of us, including Benjamin. If I had to be honest with myself, I wouldn't mind if he disappeared forever. God might strike me down for the thought, but then again, when had he intervened in my life before.

I sniffed him, only to find a hint of sandalwood, then continued to stroll around him. He distracted me from my main goal to search every inch of this place for the key. So far, all I'd found were passageways that didn't exist on the floorplan and the note sitting in my dress pocket. Its words weighed heavier than a boulder.

Ben followed—to my dismay. "What was that about?"

"I had to make sure I wasn't dealing with a drunk man. Were you gambling again?" My sharp tone hissed between the small gap in my teeth.

"How would I even be gambling here?

"You seem to find ways, dear." I strode faster. My wispy dress fluttered in my haste. I shouldn't have been so upset at my boyfriend for doing the very thing that had attracted me to him the first time we had met.

We'd been in the school parlor, all the boys betting trinkets and gold coins like water flowing from a tap. Ben had thrown down five silver towers that caught the glow of the dim light bulbs. The cocky grin of confidence he'd worn had matched his tailored suit of fine wool and flashy cufflinks.

The bells intoned in Sky Manor, cutting off my memory and echoing through the tall ceilings in the main hall. It beckoned us to dine and for a clue. I navigated through the passages, catching Rupert entering the dining room with the irritating, scholarship-girl who'd dropped out of Saint Clockwell Preparatory. If someone had to die, I'd vote for the gigglemug, but the choice didn't come from a vote. No, it came from murder and the manor's bidding.

Perhaps their affable demeanors had more to do with the elegant meal to come than their companionship. Either way, Rupert with any other girl wrung my heart out like a mop.

Ben strode toward me, almost overtaking my quick pace through the Sky Manor's main corridor. He wouldn't relent from his pursuit.

He caught my wrist and tugged me toward him. "What did you hear?"

A tingle seeped from his touch, the same sensation that invigorated me when I worked with poisons. He couldn't get enough of my inability to succumb to his deadly touch, which had been special in its time. We'd seemed meant to be, but now I longed to use the poison dangling over my bosom to subdue him, should he threaten my chance to have the treasure.

I inhaled a cool breath and dared a glance at the open doors in sight. Rupert couldn't see my interactions with Ben, who kept his lofty gaze focused on me.

"Nothing of consequence." I traced his square jaw with my finger. My daggered stare cut between my coal-coated eyelashes. It was the expression I'd given him so many times when I needed something, like silver coin or a new jewel. It showed off the better qualities of my face, I supposed. Either way, it always served its purpose.

"You're most attractive when you're mad." He lifted his chin and drew me closer.

"You're hiding something." I pushed him away.

The twitch in his cheek told me he was concealing something far worse than a failed game. Ben was proving himself a liability yet again.

"I'm going to figure out your secret, Ben." I shot like an arrow into the spacious dining room, where the loony old man had promised a clue.

A long table stretched through the middle but left us far too close to all the competitors. The idea that one of us would be dead by the next morning slithered like a snake through my midsection.

"Camilla?" Ben whispered far too loudly.

Rupert whipped his head up in my direction from his seated position around the dining room table. His easy smile was replaced with a slash across his face. My heart ached. I shifted to sit beside him, but the strange Jessie girl with her tall newsboy hat and ever-searching demeanor made me recoil. I tugged on a loose strand of hair at my neck.

Then Arden entered, smug as one might expect a banker's son. I glanced over my shoulder at Ben and gave him the *I-dare-you-to-tell-the-truth* glare. The secret had something to do with Arden. Ben's lips smashed into a firm line as he watched the banker's son, but he'd never flash his losing deck to all the players in the room. With a slight hop to my step, I took the seat beside Arden.

"Why, hello. I see you've chosen to grace me with your company." Arden undid his napkin and placed it over his lap as if he didn't have a care in the world.

Forget that he probably had heard the entirety of my argument with Ben. Forget that he had just prescribed another order of my potions like he had done so many times in school. My consolation was that whomever he chose to subdue, it wouldn't be me. I slipped into the empty chair beside him and diagonally across from Rupert.

I dropped my voice for only Arden to hear. "One, you know why I sat next to you." I spread the napkin over my lap. "Two, you promised to pay me in secrets."

Ben jerked the seat several chairs away and slammed his bottom down. "We haven't finished our conversation."

I leaned on my elbow, giving Ben a view of the back of my head.

Arden chuckled. From across the table, Rupert's jaw firmed, but he remained engaged in conversation with that gigglemug, all smiles.

"Why can't the gigglemug choke?" The question came out in a hiss.

The two across from me didn't even flinch at my comment.

Eyebrow lifted, Arden leaned closer. "Maple's a nice girl. Now, what do you have for me?" He sat back in his seat and adjusted his glasses over the bridge of his nose.

Using my free hand, I fumbled through the pocket sewn into my dress. A lady always needed easy access to her pistol and poisons. My knuckles rubbed against the note that had been left atop my vanity when I'd gone to the privy earlier in the day. The words on that strange note repeated through my mind: *You may think yourself without a flaw, but death by poison is still against the law. Careful still in how you tread because I know of Cleo and the rest of the dead.*

My fingers pinched on the slim vial and placed it into Arden's waiting palm under the table.

He snatched the vial in such a way that I questioned if the exchange even took place. His blue eyes flitted toward an automaton bringing a steaming bowl of soup.

"Follow the directions," I admonished.

Arden stuffed it into a pocket with a missive inside. The tint of yellowed paper had the same texture as the one I had received. I needed to inspect it closer. A corner of identical paper didn't mean he'd sent me the mysterious message, but with someone like Arden, it was very possible.

The old butler entered the room with frumpy pants and hair that hadn't been tamed this century. "I have the clue you've all been waiting to hear."

All heads turned in the older man's direction.

Here was my chance. I reached into Arden's trouser pocket and tore out the paper. More than one paper landed on the floor.

Arden's eyebrows furrowed. He dove to the floor and collected the contents, beating a bot to clean up his mess. The missive had the same wax seal with a crest pressed into the seal as mine.

My breath stilled in my lungs. I couldn't just sit there and let an opportunity pass. What was Arden hiding? Why would he send me such a letter? I dove to pick up a letter by the foot of my chair, but he clutched my hand.

His thumb bit into the skin around my wrist. "I have this. Thank you." Panic encased his tone.

My hands went up in surrender, and I retreated to my seat.

My note was as hard to ignore now as if it were a hot coal in all the thoughts. Yet even so, I resisted the urge to run out the room and rip it open again for any hint of who might be the sender. Was it Arden or another person who had sent a threatening note to Arden?

A buzzing automaton set a bowl of brownish soup before me, its glass eyes vacant and metallic. Another automaton across from me dropped some soup on the dolt of a girl's lap.

She yelped and giggled with the dainty air that made her cute to idiotic boys with more hormones than brain. I wanted to scream at the fellows that no one can be that nice.

And why does she keep sneaking glances across the table?

The last contestant strode through the doorway, dark and edgy, completely alluring yet so dismissive. I, at least, appreciated that he found the head of the table and ignored the apple of Rupert's eye along with the rest of us. Had he stolen an invitation like I had? All of us should have been connected somehow, yet he refused to dish out his secrets. If the poison inside Arden's pocket was meant for him, I wouldn't even need to feign dismay.

"You don't need to worry about cleaning up my messes," Rupert's friend said. "Oh, I don't want to be an inconvenience."

The automaton retreated on its giant wheel. "I apologize for the confusion," its robotic voice said. A squeaky wheel hummed through the room, cutting off conversation in its wake.

Rupert gave his irresistible smile—the one that crawled up his tan cheek and transformed his ordinary looks into someone deserving of a monument chiseled in stone. It was the same one he'd given me all those days when he'd walked me through the parks where he'd declared his love for me.

Quick tears sprouted. I dabbed at my cheeks and stood up. The dinner guests all turned in my direction for a fleeting second. The butler hadn't even shared the clue, yet my emotions got the better of me. Showing weakness wouldn't be good in front of my opponents.

"Will you excuse me?" I threw my napkin on the table. A cry quivered in my chest, but thank the heavens, it kept to its cage. My heels sank in the thick carpet with each step around the table. The double doors remained wide open and begged me to pass through. I'd return once I was composed.

"Camilla, wait," Rupert called.

I pivoted to find my beloved more handsome than ever in his finest suit jacket and with his combed hair escaping from the back of his head. Flames turned on in every sconce of the passageway, transforming the moment into something magical. Trails of warmth meandered down my cheeks and dripped from my jaw.

"Are you all right?" he asked in a note that expelled the joy I might have felt at his concern. Yet he continued to approach.

For a second, I thought he might touch my face like he used to when times were good between us.

My tongue stuck to the roof of my mouth along with the apology and declaration I hadn't the courage to say aloud. Before a word could be spoken, I had to make up my transgression against him, whether death stood at my door or I held up the scythe to take out whoever threatened to destroy him.

"You're crying." His lack of inflection agitated the boiling pot of emotions inside me.

I longed for his tender affection. Too bad his cousin had all the wealth that could solve every one of my problems.

"I-I don't know how to converse what I need to say." Converse didn't feel like the appropriate word, but I couldn't think past the streams flowing and ruining the makeup I'd painstakingly applied before dinner.

His Adam's apple bobbed. "I'm listening." The sentiment traced along every line on his face bespoke a hint of affection though he'd said he'd forsaken me.

This might be my only chance to make amends. "Rupert, I am—"

"Camilla," Ben's voice shouted from down the passage. He swaggered toward us with the confidence of a bulldog. "So, Rupert is your most recent distraction. Fitting since you both come from nothing." As he continued into the stairwell, he winked.

Why is Ben leaving when the clue hasn't even been given? He obviously wasn't overwrought with emotions like I had been. It made me want to chase him down and see what he was up to. *Does he know something I don't know? Was he planning a murder to ensure he wasn't the sacrifice for the prize?* Yet, even while accusing Ben in my thoughts, the note in my pocket burned.

Guilt trickled into my consciousness like a migraine throbbing in my skull. Rupert drew my attention with a wave of his hand. He wasn't like his cousin who would do anything to win.

"Sorry for being so late." The strange butler approached, his hair whisked back from his hurried stride. "I have the clue. Yes, I have the clue."

Rupert and I turned back toward each other, an arm's reach away. Concern pinched his eyebrows because, unlike his cousin, he had loved me in spite of all the flaws before him. His gaze lingered on the faded scar on my chin, and he smiled. A net of butterflies released in my stomach.

"Once the two out there come in, we'll start the meeting." The butler's voice was loud and suggestive, meant to lure us into the dining room.

My words came out in a whisper. "We've got to go listen to the clue." I stepped away from Rupert.

Perhaps now wasn't the time to apologize. I would win even if I flipped this mansion upside down and put the other true competitors out of commission.

Mister Woodhouse's Notes

Jessie—Dining room—8 keys
Strategy: Stealing all the keys

Arden—Dining room—1 key
Strategy: Potion collecting?

Benjamin—Dining room—1 key
Strategy: Avoiding Camilla

Camilla—Dining room—0 keys
Strategy: Rethinking alliance with Ben

Rupert—Dining room—2 keys
Strategy: Gathering information

Maple—Dining room—2 keys
*Strategy: Still proffering unwanted scones.
I (Woodhouse) may request another*

Zenith—Dining room—7 keys
Strategy: Learning more about Jessie

Vault-Hidden

CHAPTER FIVE

Rupert, the Poor Scoundrel

5:25 PM

CAMILLA SASHAYED OUT OF the corridor, taking what was left of my shattered heart with her. I knew I shouldn't still care for her. I'd only been a stepping stone in her quest for wealth, and once a better opportunity had presented itself, she'd tossed me aside like an old newspaper.

But part of me—the small part that refused to accept reality—wondered if the love we'd shared hadn't just been an act.

A few automatons rolled past me, single-minded in their duties. If only Camilla hadn't been here, I might have been just as focused.

Stupid, stupid heart. It was her fault I'd lost my money in the first place. I never would have gone to that card game if she hadn't pushed me. And when I'd spotted my well-to-do cousin Ben there, I should have known it was a bad idea. He was a Nelson, after all, and that meant he was trouble.

"The Nelson family has been broken for a long time," Father would always say when I asked him about his childhood. "The kindest thing your grandfather ever did for me was cut me out of it."

It wasn't until later I'd learned the only reason Father had been disowned was because he'd wanted to marry my mother, one of the household maids. From the little Mother had told me, Ben's father had turned out just the same.

That knowledge alone should have been enough to get my legs moving out the door before the first hand had been dealt. If only Camilla hadn't batted her eyelashes and told me I was being too uptight, that there was no harm in having a bit of fun. Especially when it could have gotten us enough money for the lavish wedding she'd always dreamed of.

But that was Camilla. Always looking for what could be gained, never satisfied with what she already had. Including me.

I could hardly fault her, though, knowing where she'd come from. How I'd longed to ease that frightened spirit of hers, help her find the security she'd always lacked. But before I'd been able to, she'd sweet-talked me into throwing my money down the drain, then run straight into my cousin's open arms.

Now she'd gone and gotten herself into more trouble.

I stared at the spot in the hall where she'd stood only moments ago, wondering if I should try talking to her again. Perhaps after we'd listened to Woodhouse's clue, she'd be more keen on confiding in me.

Camilla's not the only one I need to talk to. I also needed to confront Arden Bentley and find out just what my former girlfriend had passed him under the table. I hadn't been able to see it from my seat, but the devilish grin on the man's face had nearly made my stomach turn.

I hadn't had any personal dealings with him, but I knew he and Camilla had gone to Saint Clockwell Preparatory Academy together. I'd asked her once what their relationship was, but she'd just laughed and told me not to worry about it.

Ha, as if not worrying is an option when it comes to her.

"Are you quite all right, sir?" asked an automaton as it came up beside me. "Would you like me to tell Mr. Woodhouse you won't be returning for the meeting?"

"No, I was just about to come back."

The automaton nodded its mechanical head, said a quick, "Very good, sir," and rolled off. I marched back into the dining room, my gaze locking with Arden's as I sat down beside Maple.

When he raised a quizzical eyebrow, I mouthed, "I'll talk to you after," then looked up at Woodhouse, whose hands were clenched around a sheet of paper.

"Is everything okay?" Maple whispered. She glanced between Arden and me, her features drawn together in concern.

"Of course." I smiled to ease her suspicions, then asked, "What was it you were telling me about the rooms? They have hidden doors?"

Her expression lifted. "Ah, yes—well, mine did, anyway. I haven't figured out how to solve the riddle I found once I opened it though." Her brown eyes glazed over for a moment, then she giggled. "I suppose I shouldn't be telling you everything since we're competitors." She sipped her drink.

"I understand. I suppose I'll need to take a closer look around my room to see if there's anything interesting in it."

Truth be told, I'd already searched my bedroom with a fine-toothed comb. The sculptures, oil paintings, and mantel had seemed like likely hiding spots, so I'd searched them first. When they hadn't produced results, I'd moved on to the fireplace itself, then the rugs, wallpaper, and doorframes. I'd even cut open my mattress to make sure nothing had been hidden among the box springs. Our host wouldn't be happy when that was discovered, but in a game like this, I wasn't about to overlook something for the sake of manners.

Though I'd learned my lesson about gambling, I would have bet my life there wasn't a key in my room. I may have been a tad rusty, but there were some skills you never lost.

Those skills *had* proven handy when I'd checked the bottom side of this grand table earlier and collected a slender silver key. It was sitting safely in my left trouser pocket right now. *Could this be the one that opens the vault?*

Woodhouse cleared his throat and raised an eyebrow at Maple and me, silently scolding us for chatting when he was about to make his announcement. "All right, the clue is . . . "

"To find the key and vault you seek

You must first prove your mettle

Lay aside your honor and pride

Victory awaits at the lowest level."

"Lowest level? Does that mean—" Camilla started to ask.

"Wait, I'm not finished," Woodhouse cut in.

"Though beware, contestants, there are many keys

Collect them as you will

But until a competitor's lifeblood is spilled

No treasure shall you seize."

Everyone looked around the table at each other, taking in the butler's words. Dread seemed to settle over the large dining room like spider threads, wrapping us too tightly for any chance of escape. The flickering flames in the chandelier seemed dimmer now, matching the somber atmosphere of the room.

"You mean, the keys won't even work until someone dies?" Maple's voice was almost a high-pitched squeak.

"That's correct." Woodhouse tucked the paper back into his jacket, completely at ease despite the clue's gruesome contents.

"What happens if no one dies by the end of the time?"

The old man hesitated, then glanced at the automatons stationed by the door. "Sky Manor is very . . . persuasive."

He excused himself with a bow, but the rest of us hardly noticed as we gulped down the clear gravy soup, stewed eels, and curried lobster with rice the automatons placed before us. The game was on, and I could tell from the other competitors' expressions that they were just as anxious to get back to searching as I was.

After I meet with Arden. I gave the fellow another pointed look to make sure he didn't forget.

Once our dessert of blancmange was finished, I made a point of excusing myself to freshen up in my room, hoping Arden would follow. When a sharp knock sounded at my door a few minutes later, I let him inside.

"What's this about?" he asked, clearly unhappy at being summoned. He tapped his fingers against his pants leg.

"What did Camilla give you under the table?" My voice came out a tad more desperate than I intended, but perhaps that would push him to give me a straight answer.

He took a step back, then slowly pulled a glowing blue vial out of his pocket. "Ah, you must mean this. A simple tonic she whipped up recently. I get terrible headaches."

"A tonic? Are you sure? That color seems . . ." I reached for the vial, but Arden returned it to his jacket pocket.

"I'm not in the habit of sharing, you know."

Something dark twisted in my gut. "Are you talking about the tonic or Camilla? Last I checked, she makes her own choices about whom she wants to be with. And it's not you."

His mouth quirked up into a dry smile. "You've got this all wrong. She and I are business partners. Have been for quite some time."

I frowned. "What? Business partners? What kind of—" My stomach dropped as I recalled a conversation Camilla and I had had while strolling in the park. The day before things had ended between us.

She'd always had a fascination with flowers and, as a Chemistry major, had loved telling me about their medicinal properties. On this particular morning, she'd been strangely quiet. I'd asked her several questions and only gotten vague, halfhearted answers. I didn't want to push her, but something was definitely bothering her.

As we came up to a cluster of deep blue flowers, she bent down and traced her fingers over their delicate petals. A faint smile formed on her lips, her eyes going distant. "It's funny how many things seem harmless, but when used the right way, they can actually prove deadly. Did you know larkspur is fatal to humans? Such a beautiful, unassuming thing. How easy it would be . . ."

"Camilla?"

She slowly rose back up and turned to me. "Yes, my love?"

I took her hands in mine. "Did something happen? You seem . . . upset."

Camilla shook her head with a laugh. "Oh, Rupert, you say the funniest things. I'm completely fine. But I do enjoy how you worry over me."

"Only because I love you," I said earnestly. "If there was something wrong, you would tell me, wouldn't you?" I peered into her lovely brown eyes, hoping she knew I would do anything—*anything*—to keep her safe.

"Of course."

We'd left the park shortly after that, but I'd noticed how she'd slipped a few larkspur petals into her bag. Petals the same shade as the "tonic" in Arden's pocket.

It can't be that Camilla took her skills and turned to poison, can it? Her family had always been strapped for money; she'd shared as much in one of her more vulnerable moments, and I'd done what I could to help them live comfortably while we were together.

Surely she wouldn't do something like that.

But here we were in the middle of a game that we knew would end in someone's death. *Was the promise of wealth too tempting?*

"What kind of business partners?" I asked, trying to keep my voice from shaking.

Arden's face became stony. "I don't believe I need to answer that question. Now, you must excuse me; I have other matters to attend to." With that, he swept out of the room, too self-important to waste more time on a fool like me.

Perhaps I was a fool, but I wasn't about to let Camilla's desperation drive her to do something she'd regret.

Even if it meant resorting to a life I'd sworn I was done with.

I sat down at my desk and penned a note, then went to the door and called for the nearest automaton to deliver it.

Mister Woodhouse's Notes

Jessie—Main atrium—9 keys
Strategy: Thievery. Skillfully done.

Arden—Second floor passage—1 key
Strategy: Riling up more contestants. Purposefully?
Yet to be determined.

Benjamin—Snooping outside Rupert's bedroom—1 key
Strategy: Avoiding Camilla

Camilla—West stairwell—1 key
Strategy: Blackmail?

Rupert—His bedroom—2 keys
Strategy: Attempted alliance with Arden? Sent an
automaton off with a note. Love letter to Camilla or
something more sinister?

Maple—East stairwell—2 keys
Strategy: Keeping secrets, further exploring

Zenith—Rooftop—10 keys
Strategy: Avoiding Jessie, she's far too distracting

Vault-Hidden

Chapter Six

Jessie, the Thief

6:30 PM

In a nook with pink wallpaper and wooden molding hiding me in its shadows, I waited for Arden to depart Rupert's room. I couldn't hear their exchange, but noticed the strange blue bottle being slipped back into Arden's pocket, the very one Camilla had handed him when she'd thought no one was looking. Arden closed the door and meandered through the center of the wide passage. I followed his long stride.

He turned his head in my direction.

This was my opportunity to talk. "What did you think of our clue?" I clasped and unclasped my hands, unsure how to broach the actual conversation I wanted to have with him.

"You mean the long-winded poem that said what we already knew?" He chuckled. "It seems we have a murder to plan."

"So, it does." The words spilled out of my mouth before I realized I'd just agreed to plan a murder. No, I was supposed to be fixing my life, not adding to my list of crimes. "What is it? Poison, poison darts, a butter knife to the throat?" I inwardly cringed at my terrible joke. He had to know I was joking.

His eyebrows furrowed with suspicion.

"Would you like to search this room with me?" I asked.

Arden's crystal blue eyes flashed with surprise before he wrestled his expression into an amused grin. He gestured to a door. "Sure, I don't have a better plan."

"Maybe I really did bring my poison darts and have you where I want you." My fists clenched at the last statement.

He paused mid-step and looked down his nose at me, a question arching his eyebrows. "I have some business to finish. Save those poison darts for Ben or even Camilla if you like." The monotone voice almost made me miss the glint of mischief behind his spectacles.

When he entered the room, I inhaled deeply, catching a hint of cedarwood and another floral aroma drifting from Arden. I'd have to uncover what business he had at this game and if he knew about me.

The parlor room we entered had portraits hanging on the walls, a fireplace, upholstered chairs, and giant windows, which let in late afternoon sunlight through sheer curtains.

Arden reached for the suspended material, checking between the layers of cloth. "How about you take that side and we'll meet by the fireplace?"

"Does that make us allies?" I asked.

"For now."

"You don't have a pistol in that coat jacket?" I backstepped, realizing that though I longed to hug him and, dare I say, love him, he hadn't a clue I was his sister.

"Don't worry. I only plan to shoot Benjamin, should he enter without my permission." He tipped his head down, still wearing the slightest hint of a grin. He shifted, opening his jacket enough to reveal a strap and a pistol-sized bulge beneath his jacket.

The threat was real. When the floorboards creaked at the doorway, we both whipped our heads to the intruder.

For a split second, my heart dropped. I imagined Benjamin's blond hair entering, but instead, a bronze automaton rolled across the threshold of the doorway.

"Miss Jessie Smith, a message for you." The robotic voice rang like a music box, clinking with each note. The metallic arm stretched upward, offering a paper note with its clamp for a hand.

Arden met my gaze, then continued inspecting a portrait of a morose young girl dressed in the styles popular a century ago.

I grabbed the note and read the letters. Blood drained from my cheeks. "Will you excuse me?" The words slipped out from the shock of the letters scrawled on the page and my deep longing.

"Jessie?" Arden called after me, but I squeezed between the automaton and the wall.

"I'll be back." My feet didn't stop moving until I'd fled up a level to the tower I'd claimed as my quarters for the night. Stretched across the bed was the pink dress I'd stolen from Camilla and a skeleton key I'd never seen before.

It was as if the manor had rewarded me for stealing. The pounding in my chest intensified with the temptation to continue this game and delve deeper into my crimes by helping the old chum I'd once called a friend.

A small desk leaned against the wall by the door. I picked up a dip pen and twisted open a glass inkwell. Even the designs on the lid bespoke wealth and the lavish lifestyle I'd always envied.

Even so, the words of the matrons at my old orphanage splattered through my memory, pointing to how God had provided for me even in my poverty. I slid open the desk drawer and lifted a single creamy page. Somehow, the paper grew heavier with the weight of the decision I had to make.

My gaze lifted to a portrait across the room with haunted, dark eyes that observed my every move. An icy chill shivered down my back. I steeled my nerves, dipped the pen into the inkwell, and wrote.

Mister Woodhouse's Notes

Jessie—3rd floor bedroom—9 keys
Strategy: Multiple alliances and thievery perhaps?

Arden—Second floor passage—1 key
Strategy: Switching up from making rivals to making friends?

Benjamin—Snooping outside Camilla's bedroom—1 key
Strategy: Avoiding Camilla

Camilla—West stairwell—0 keys
Strategy: Broken alliance; she seems to be haphazardly searching after her keys went missing.

Rupert—Upstairs Bathroom—2 keys
Strategy: Avoiding spider bites

Maple—Second floor passage—2 keys
Strategy: Exploring the halls. Hunting Arden?

Zenith—Hidden dumbwaiter—13 keys
Strategy: Unnerving everyone, including me (Woodhouse)

Vault-Hidden

CHAPTER SEVEN

Rupert, the Poor Scoundrel

6:55 PM

I'D JUST FINISHED SEARCHING the bathroom nearest my quarters—without finding anything of note besides a couple of spiders—when the automaton returned, a new note in hand.

"For you, sir." The machine's dead eyes remained straight ahead rather than meeting mine. I'd not had much experience with automatons before. Most people said they were fairly harmless, unless you happened to trip over one. I wasn't so sure.

When it didn't leave after I took the message, I cleared my throat, hoping it would get the hint to move along. I wasn't about to read with that thing potentially looking over my shoulder.

"I am waiting in case you would like me to send another letter."

I repressed a shudder at its mechanical voice. "That won't be necessary. Carry on with your duties."

"Very good, sir." It disappeared down the hall, but even so, I slipped back into my bedroom to make sure I truly was alone before reading the message.

You told me before that our arrangement was over. Don't contact me again.

I crumpled the note and tossed it in the bedroom's wastebasket. If Jessie wouldn't help me, I'd have to find another solution.

Light sparkled near the bed beneath the mahogany rug. That most definitely hadn't been there before. I leaped from my chair. *Another key?* Hope and apprehension mingled in my gut. If it was the right one, I'd be one step closer to finishing this twisted game and rescuing Camilla from whatever she'd gotten herself caught up in.

Instead, I grasped a letter, enclosed with a thick wax seal. The wax was golden, imprinted with a strange insignia. I ripped it open, then dropped it as soon as I'd read the contents.

Just because your dirty money is gone, did you really think no one would find out where it came from?

Fear slithered down my spine. *What is this? Blackmail or just someone trying to scare me?*

And how did they find out? I've been so careful. . . .

On a wild impulse, I retrieved the note I'd tossed into the wastebasket and held the two messages up next to each other. It was a farfetched theory, but I needed to be sure.

The handwriting was starkly different, making it clear Jessie wasn't behind the second note. I berated myself for even considering such a notion. I knew I'd wounded her when I'd ended our partnership, but she wasn't the type of person to turn on me like that.

Especially not when I could easily take her down with me.

But if she wasn't behind the second message, that meant someone else knew my secret.

My hands shook as I tucked both notes into my trouser pocket. This game had gotten very serious very quickly. I couldn't afford for the truth to come out; otherwise, I'd wind up on the inside of a prison cell. Better to die than rot in there for the rest of my life.

But the note didn't mention any demands, so until I figured out who had written it, there was nothing I could do to ensure my secret stayed buried.

My thoughts strayed back to the clue Woodhouse had given us. *"Victory awaits at the lowest level." Is the vault in the basement? Or was that little detail just a trick to throw us off?* If it was a red herring, I might go hunting in the wrong place and end up wasting the little time I had left.

I had two keys right now, but from the jingling the other contestants made as they walked by, my odds didn't look too good that I'd be able to open the vault if I happened to find it.

And don't forget that the "right" key won't even work until one of us dies. I dragged a hand down my face. I'd learned how to defend myself in a fistfight after being targeted in school for having my mother's dark complexion. But if someone attacked me with a weapon, I doubted I'd be the winner.

And what about Camilla? If that "tonic" is what I think it is, she's about to make a mistake she can't come back from.

I picked up the knife I'd used to slice open my mattress and turned it over in my hands a few times. *Maybe I should rethink this. . . .*

I threw open the door and sauntered out with a smile. My mood was far from fair, but I needed to keep up appearances. I'd always been good at going unnoticed, though I hadn't needed that skill nearly as much since I'd gone straight.

I could only hope I was still good enough to pull off one last hit.

Mister Woodhouse's Notes

Jessie—Second floor—10 keys
Strategy: Wow! The manor loves her.

Arden—Second floor passage—1 key
Strategy: Back to searching through plants. An herbologist in our midst.

Benjamin—Parlor—1 key
Strategy: Still avoiding others, not finding anything

Camilla—West stairwell—0 keys
Strategy: No strategy besides making a mess. The automatons are going wild.

Rupert—Just outside his bedroom—2 keys
Strategy: Unknown, but the look in his eyes suggests trouble.

Maple—Second-floor passage—2 keys
Strategy: Definitely hunting Arden. Getting warmer

Zenith—Second floor—12 keys
Strategy: Keeping a close eye on Jessie, just in case

Vault-Hidden

Chapter Eight

Maple, the Nice Girl

Roughly 7:00 PM

Where did he go?

I hurried my pace through the cheerfully pink hallways. I couldn't help but wonder who had designed the decor. But, of course, no one knew where this manor came from, much less its decorations. All we knew was that the game offered a chance at a new life. If only one could find a key . . . and survive.

I knew better than to get my hopes up. I wasn't the kind of girl who won contests like these. But at least I was good at surviving. All I needed to do was smile, stay out of other people's way, and be the nice girl everyone already knew me to be. Like Father used to say, "Maple sweet, there's not a hateful bone in your body."

I shoved the memory from my mind and brought my task back into focus. I could think about the contest later, on the slim chance I might win, but it was time to find the *real* reason I'd been so thrilled at the invitation to the competition: Arden Bentley.

My friend had been the best thing about my old life at Saint Clockwell Preparatory Academy. After everything had collapsed, he had become my one regret about losing that scholarship. Sure, I'd also lost the chance at a better life, which my diploma could have brought, or a possibility at earning a university scholarship, but I had long since accepted that such a life wasn't for me. The other students at school had made that clear. All except Arden. And I needed to find him.

With everyone else around, there had not been any chance to say hi without drawing unwelcome attention. I'd thought we might finally connect when he had peeked into the library, but he had left so quickly—perhaps he hadn't seen me. I shook my head. He had looked right at me before he'd rushed away. I wanted to believe he'd just been distracted. Part of me wondered if he was avoiding our reunion, but that didn't match the boy I remembered.

I clutched my bag of peach scones and rushed around the corner of the next hall, slamming into another body. The collision sent me and the other poor soul crashing to the carpeted floor. The bag flew from my hands in the other direction. I turned my head while falling, watching, as if time had slowed. One of the scones spilled out and crumbled onto the ground. To my relief, only one was lost.

I regathered my wits and glanced toward the mess of limbs and red fabric that made up whatever girl I'd inconvenienced. "I'm so awfully sorry. I wasn't paying—"

Wait, was that a gun by her side?

All feelings left my body as a face red with fury and a high voice to match it rose from the pile of fabric. "What are you trying to do to me, you unworthy gnat?" she shrieked as she snatched up the gun, hiding it beneath the skirts she readjusted.

Camilla. I inwardly pleaded with heaven that she didn't recognize me from school. Surely, it had been long enough since I'd dropped out of that wretched place. I briefly considered asking about the deadly weapon she'd tried to hide.

"I can't apprehend how you managed to get yourself an invitation to this thing, but you better stay out of my way," she seethed. "You don't belong here. You belong with all the other lowborn dogs."

Staring at the carpet, I resisted the urge to scoff at her use of *apprehend* when she must have meant *comprehend*. Nice girls don't mock other people's misuse of words, I reminded myself.

But she made me wish I wasn't a *nice girl*. No. She made me remember I wasn't.

Something deep within me, something horrifying and awful, began to stir. No. No, no, no, no, no. Not now. Not here. Not again.

My eyes squeezed shut and I held my breath, trying to drown out her grating voice and stifle whatever it was inside me trying to rear its ugly head.

I will not give in.

"What happened here?"

The inner monsters fled at the sound of a friendly voice, and I glanced up to see Rupert walking toward us from the opposite end of the hall.

Camilla took a turn being dumbstruck. Her face drained of color before she clamped her mouth shut. She gave me one last glare, then slipped around the corner.

"Camilla, wait," Rupert called after her. He ran past me and stopped short where the hall turned. He stood aghast. "She's disappeared," he half-whispered.

Rupert glanced my way where I still floundered on the floor. His eyes widened as he reached a hand down to help me up. "Sorry, I didn't see you. Are you all right?"

"Thank you, I'm fine." I noted the pained look in his eye as it wandered back toward where Camilla had fled, and remembered how he'd gone after her when she'd left the dining hall. Yet, I couldn't fathom what a nice guy like Rupert had to do with such a venomous person.

"Do you know that—" a rude name crossed my mind, but I shooed it away "—girl?" I leaned down to rescue my bag of scones.

Rupert's eyes fell to the floor. "She and I— We—" he faltered. "We were together."

I only stared. It wasn't a picture I could imagine. "As in, dated?"

He nodded. "But our relationship ended when my fortune did. Soon after, she started dating my *wealthy cousin*." His voice held a bitter edge. "I keep telling myself I'm well past all that." His eyes trailed again toward the direction she'd fled, those last words seeming more to himself than to me.

I stood, clutching the recovered peach scones, and bit back my instinctual advice that anyone would be better off without her. He was obviously hurting, and those words would do nothing to console him. I glanced around, trying to think of the right words, when my eyes fell back to the precious bag in my hands. Those scones could cheer anyone up.

"Are you sure you don't want one of these?" I lifted the bag. "I swear, they're the pride of the Screaming Peach Café. I've worked pretty hard to perfect the recipe, and my boss has made them our signature treat."

He gave a half-hearted smile. "That's nice of you, Maple. But I haven't got much of an appetite. I should probably get back to the competition, anyway."

Right, the competition. So far, everyone except Mr. Woodhouse had rejected my peace offering. It had probably been a bad idea to bring them. The truth was, I only wanted to share one with Arden when I saw him again. He knew about my love for baking and had always encouraged me. But I also didn't want to be rude to everyone else. I should have known most of them would feel suspicious of food from a fellow competitor.

I shrugged it off. "Okay, but you're missing out."

He gave a sad smile and nod before turning to leave.

"Wait." I pulled his attention back. "Maybe you don't know him, but I'm looking for the banker's son, Arden Bentley. Have you seen him anywhere?"

Rupert's face darkened. His eyes glared toward the wall as he bit out his words. "I'd stay away from Arden Bentley if I were you."

I stepped back in surprise. Perhaps I wasn't the only one fighting inner monsters. "He's an old friend of mine," I tried to explain.

"Trust me." Rupert turned, adding before his departure, "Arden Bentley is a friend to no one."

Alone again in the halls, I tried to reconcile Rupert's words with the boy I remembered from Chemistry class. Rupert seemed nice enough. What could have possibly put enmity between him and someone as wonderful as Arden?

I thought back to the way Rupert had spoken so bitterly of Camilla's relationship with his cousin. The connection brought my mind back to the way Camilla had sat so close to Arden in the dining hall. My stomach dropped at the sickening realization. If Camilla had left Rupert to be with the wealthier cousin, what would stop her from leaving Ben to chase after Arden?

Fear twisted in my gut, wrapping together with the eagerly awaiting darkness I so desperately tried to tamp down. I leaned against the wall, recalling every cruel and bitter word Camilla had thrown at me. The dark tendrils crept up into my chest, tightening around my heart, threatening to take over my will. My pulse pounded in my ears, silencing my protests. I could get over mere words. But I couldn't get over her sinking her claws into dear Arden.

A gentle hand on my shoulder stilled the inward battle, and the darkness fled back to some recess within me. I turned with a start, and encountered a kind old face peering into mine. "Everything all right, miss?"

Woodhouse. The mysterious butler of this place. Something about the compassionate spark in his eye and the soft tone of his voice chased away awful shadows of fear. I took a calming breath.

What was I worried about? Arden would never associate himself with the likes of Camilla.

"I was hoping to find my friend. He's one of the competitors, Arden Bentley. Have you seen him?"

"As a matter of fact, I just did." Woodhouse gave a knowing grin. He pointed to the ceiling. "Just follow the vines, and you'll find him."

Finally tasting hope, I looked up. Green vines curled into the ceiling design, seeming to point in one direction down the hall. Curious, had that been there before?

"Thank you." I glanced back toward Woodhouse with appreciation, but the butler had already left. I recalled his mention of hidden passages. He must have run off to keep up with all the other guests wandering around.

I followed the vines, surprised when they led me back toward the library, where I had almost caught a moment alone with Arden a few hours before. I gently pushed the door open, grateful that it didn't creak. Arden's back faced me. He stood at a shelf and meticulously removed a small stack of books, pressing on the shelf behind them. Then he placed that stack back on the shelf and moved on to the next stack. Did he believe he'd find a key back there? I smiled at his methodic determination. He hadn't changed a bit. His discerning eyes were always careful to take in every detail in his surroundings, making him the perfect chemistry partner, and an especially perceptive friend. He'd somehow always picked up when I felt nervous or unsettled, and found little ways to set me at ease or make me smile, as if he had studied my mannerisms the same way he now studied those shelves.

I slipped into the room, unsure of what to say to someone I had waited so long to see again. My foot scuffed over the library's hardwood floor, and he whirled around, pulling the book back as if ready to throw it at me. I froze. So did he. We both stood staring at one another for what felt like an age until, finally, he glanced toward the door behind me.

"Sorry, miss, I must be on edge." He lowered the book, taking on a more relaxed stance.

I furrowed my brow. He'd called me "miss," like he had when we'd first met in chemistry class. We'd been assigned as partners on the first day of school. I had thought it was strange the way the wealthy students were taught to address strangers even from a young age. We'd been in high school for goodness' sake. I'd teased him about it endlessly after.

I shook my head as my mind blanked. I glanced around the room, trying to remember what I'd planned to say. All I could think about was the paper bag of scones, the top of which was now fisted in my hand. I raised it. "Scone?"

My offer must have caught him off guard. He stared at the bag, appearing to debate his answer. Finally, he spoke. "That sounds . . . delightful."

I opened the bag and offered it to him.

He reached in, pulled out a slightly smushed scone, and took a bite without hesitation. Within seconds, his features lit up. "This might be the most magnificent thing I've ever tasted."

I beamed with pride. Seeing his delight gave a lift to my confidence. "I'm so glad you like it. It's really great to see you."

Right before taking another bite, Arden paused and lowered the scone. He knitted his brow. "Forgive me, I don't think I caught your name on the zeppelin over here."

My heart sank. My name? I hadn't mentioned my name on the zeppelin, I'd been too busy avoiding everyone else. But how could he not remember me when I was standing right here in front of him? It *had* been two years since I'd abandoned my scholarship after Father's passing, so I could support Mother. And I'd only attended the school my freshman year and half of my sophomore year. But we'd been so close at the time. I guessed we all looked different.

An awkward laugh slipped from my lips, and I couldn't help hearing the pain in my own voice. "It's Maple." Perhaps after hearing my name, he'd connect the dots.

He straightened. "What a lovely name." He lifted the scone as if making a toast. "Thank you for sharing your wonderful scones. You have a great gift."

My throat tightened, choking back any possible response. My vision swam as heat flooded my face, replacing my pride with complete mortification. I'd been certain he'd be as happy to see me as I'd been to see him.

"I hope you'll excuse me, Miss Maple. I must get back to the competition." He abandoned his hunt through the bookshelves to step around me. He reached for the door, and then stopped, not turning back. Had my identity registered in his mind?

"Perhaps we can meet again—when this is all over," Arden said in a low voice before slipping out the door.

Unable to move, unable to think, I stared blindly at the shelves. My feet stuck to the library floor until my knees buckled and I doubled over. Tears blocked my vision before streaming down my cheeks.

The paper bag dropped from my hands, and I fell to my knees, half-crushing the scones that remained. What did they matter anymore? He'd forgotten. The playful smiles, the inside jokes, the way it had sometimes felt like it was us against the world. Had I just been a passing distraction to him? He'd been my world when I was there. My safe place. Circumstances had made it impossible for us to see each other afterward. But the invitation to this game had been like a lifeline. My chance to tell him I still thought about him every day.

What a heartsick fool I'd been. Of course he wouldn't have given the scholarship girl a second thought. What had I expected? Our lives were worlds apart. But I thought he was different. I'd believed it with every fiber of my being, and look where it had gotten me.

He was just like the rest of them.

For the third time, my quiet reasoning became silenced by a swirl of chaos within me. My heart pounded painfully in my chest, as I lost all strength and will to push down the hidden darkness which rose from my gut, wrapped around my chest and took over my thoughts. No one else was here to stop it, either. I'd wasted hours of this competition already, small talking with one contestant while pining over another. I didn't need them. I didn't need any of them.

I needed to win this contest. What would this lot of rich snobs do with the prize when they already had everything? A nudge of a thought reminded me I wasn't the only contestant trapped in poverty, but I shoved it away. That line of thinking would do nothing to help me win. Mother and I needed this prize more than everyone else.

Arden wouldn't forget me then. But it would be too late. I'd win this contest, no matter the cost.

When Father used to tell me I didn't have a hateful bone in my body, I never had the heart to tell him he was wrong. I battled with hate every day. The one time I'd let it win, I'd lived to regret it ever since. But today, I let the hate win again.

I wiped my eyes and hardened my features, before feeling in my pocket for the extra key I hadn't given much thought about since I'd discovered it in the secret compartment in my room—I'd told Rupert I'd found a clue instead of revealing my early luck in the game. Perhaps part of me had known I'd commit to this deadly competition, after all.

I stood and opened the door.

A flash of black fabric passed me by, and some sort of paper dropped to the ground behind the figure. I leaned into the hallway to try and identify which competitor might have overheard my exchange with Arden. Reaching down to pick up an envelope, I nearly called after the disappearing stranger that they'd dropped something, but I stopped myself. *What if this was their clue?* I glared down at the envelope, turning it over to find a gold wax seal. *Then it can only help me. No more nice girl.*

I broke the seal and opened the note, then stared at the terrifying words.

Maple sweet, as sweet as honey
Making up for lack of money
But sweetness can't forever hide
The darkness lurking deep inside

Mister Woodhouse's Notes

Jessie—North side of the second floor—11 keys
Strategy: Clutch your pockets. We've got a thief.

Arden—Second floor passage—1 key
Strategy: Snacks and lies

Benjamin—Looking for my room—1 key
Strategy: Failing at everything

Camilla—Her bedroom—0 keys
Strategy: Just noticed the missing dress; the rage is palpable

Rupert—Second floor hallway—2 keys
Strategy: Trying not to look suspicious. What is he up to?

Maple—Library—2 keys
Strategy: Destroying and abandoning her scones. What a shame.

Zenith—Main library—14 keys
Strategy: Keeping ahead of Jessie's key count

Vault-Hidden

CHAPTER NINE

Zenith, the Outsider

20:00

"A POX ON ALL of your houses." I stuffed the dossier back into the inner pocket of my black leather jacket with a grimace, careful not to allow my collection of keys to jingle. My coat was the only personal article of clothing I wore. To play the part, and fit in with the other attendees, I'd been forced into a stiff, high-collared dress shirt to conceal my tattoos. I'd begun the inking process young, earning the first marks when I was eight, shortly after the death of my mother. If seen, their number would reveal my age despite my youthful face, disqualifying me from participating in the game.

"Zenith." I rolled my eyes, pulling the small listening device my employer had delivered with the dossier from around my neck and held the shiny brass coil to my ear.

"Listening." I kept my response clipped and leaned back into the shadows, a chameleon shifting into my natural environment.

"I have been waiting for your report. Have you secured the win?" Greed dripped from the man's voice.

"Our agreement was to guard your son's life, was it not?" Sarcasm was a card best played when I had an advantage, and from my current vantage point, all the cards were securely at my disposal.

"Yes," he growled. "But the best way to ensure his safety is if he's in possession of the treasure. None would dare to touch him then. This is my son we're talking about."

I had certainly not forgotten about his son. Arden had been a constant in my thoughts since the day I'd learned his conception had sealed my mother's doom. It was Mr. Bentley who had forgotten about me, and the revenge I would exact on the stage he had set could not have been more poetic.

"He still breathes." I shoved the device under my stiff shirt and ignored the squawking protests of my employer, letting them fade beneath the squeak of my leather jacket as I stepped into the hallway.

My hand drifted to my hair, and I brushed it from my forehead. It had grown a tad too long, leaving me looking like a raven in need of preening. While solid memories of my mother were few, I'd never forgotten the way she'd referred to my hair as raven's wings. An image of her laughing face and dancing eyes as she tousled my hair was the one I always came back to when I needed to keep my head on straight. An obsession with birds and a proclivity for knives were the two gifts she'd bestowed on me before falling victim to love, a mistake I'd determined not to make. No amount of Camilla's fluttering, Jessie's wit, or Maple's peach scones would sway me on this mission.

I chastised myself for allowing the other players to get under my skin. They weren't all that bad. Okay, given what I knew about them, any one of them could be tipped over the precipice and enticed to murder. And the banker had made certain I had everything I needed to push them in that direction, as long as it edged them away from Arden and his ability to add to his father's coffers.

But my mission was clear. Regardless of the sum the banker had paid me at the onset, Arden was on his own. Let them claw at one another's necks. I'd find the key and be rid of them before they realized I was gone.

The cogs of my watch clicked the time away. I glanced at the timepiece, the initials etched on the case snagging my eyes as they always did. But I had no time for being sentimental. Punctuality was a skill I had to learn early on in my career, and the reason I always preferred using a twenty-four hour clock.

Nothing could be worse than showing up for an assignment at ten in the morning when the actual target was not scheduled to arrive until ten at night, and all because of imprecise timing.

Five minutes until my meeting with Woodhouse. The banker had given me more than sufficient funds to bribe the eccentric scientist, but that was another sum I'd easily been able to spirit away into my own pocketbook. The missive I'd extracted from his estranged daughter had earned me the old man's trust instantly. I still couldn't quite believe my luck with that one. She'd just so happened to be captaining the zeppelin that carried us to Sky Manor, a fact that had quickly assured me she'd maintained a soft spot for her quirky father.

I made my way along the hallway toward the back stairs, catching glimpses of several other players as I headed toward the basement. I'd already dismissed half the rooms on this level as potential hiding places for the safe. There was no reason to linger.

An ancient bot with reversed hands stood at the entrance to the stairway. Whether Woodhouse expected him to act as a guard or simply unnerve anyone curious about the lower floor, I barely gave the decrepit pile of rusty metal a glance.

"Ah, you're here." Woodhouse didn't bother looking up when I reached the bottom of the stairs. He was bent over a table covered in springs and cogs, fiddling with a contraption I didn't recognize. The thick lenses of his oversized goggles gave him the appearance of a mechanical owl. "I should have realized you were the punctual type."

I had no need for pleasantries. He'd already accepted my deal. I slipped the second page of his daughter's missive across the table, sending a handful of springs bouncing to the floor.

"The codes." He slid a battered, blue notebook over to me, careful not to disturb his mess of bits and tools. "They change every half-turn of the clock."

Thumbing through the sheets, I studied the cramped scribbling. He hadn't bothered to make anything easy for me, but I'd sort it out later. I gave a nod he might or might not see and spun back to the stairs, the chain of my pocket watch clanking against the handle of one of my blades—the one I'd left visible as a silent reminder that I wasn't to be trifled with.

Back at the top of the stairs, I spotted a flash of red velvet and black lace trim, the telltale sign that Camilla had recently vacated the hallway. Judging by how quickly the dress swayed, she was chasing someone, but I couldn't be certain whether it was Benjamin or not. At the rate she'd been passing out smiles, I had a feeling she'd move on to Arden the instant she got a whiff of Ben's real bank statement. Although the spark in her eyes when she thought no one was watching her gaze shift to Rupert told me there was more to the story between them.

I reached into the pocket of my jacket and felt the edge of my final delivery. Every detail had been planned out by my employer. He'd done his research perfectly on every player, even the ones who thought they'd made it to Sky Manor of their own accord, but he'd failed to dig into my past. He thought he'd hired a shadow, an outsider with no skin in the game, willing to accept his money and maintain anonymity. My impeccable reputation had been enough to tempt him and blind him to why I'd eliminated every other likely candidate for the job so I could be here in person. It was the reason I'd delivered a message to his son, the same as I had to everyone else. Maybe the time he'd spent with my mother had meant so little to him that having her killed had erased her from his memory, but I would never forgive him for taking her from me.

I ticked through what I knew about the other players in sync with the ticking of my timepiece, sorting out the best ways to deal with them once my messages had time to work their magic. Jessie had already been trying to figure out the best way to reveal her relationship to Arden. I'd seen the discomfort in her eyes when she'd looked at him on the zeppelin. It was a feeling I was familiar with. Knowing those responsible for your suffering have lived in carefree comfort while you've been forced to find your way tasted like ash and radishes. I felt an odd kinship to her, but that hadn't stopped me from giving her the note revealing her heists were not as secret as she wanted to believe. It was only a pity that this had lost me a key or two to her sleight of hand.

Even if I hadn't been made aware of Maple's darker dealings, her perpetual attempts to play up her old friendship with Arden and make friends with the other players by offering them homemade baked goods would have been enough to tell me she was hiding a deeper darkness. When I'd passed her on the stairs, her eyes had grown shiftier. She was nervous, and the jumpier she got, the more likely she was to make a mistake and reveal the truth. If I cared about protecting Arden, I'd be watching her more closely.

A door opened down the hall, interrupting my thoughts. Rupert stepped out and scanned the hallway in both directions, but I'd already stepped into the shadows, my chameleon coat blending seamlessly into the darkness. A flash of bright fabric swirled around him. It appeared that Camilla was making her move. I held back a satisfied chuckle. Ben's secrets weren't going to stay hidden for long. They'd be swapping alliances like limited edition trading cards before the Sky Manor clock tolled midnight, and I was determined to make my move long before then.

The pair vanished behind another set of doors, and I slipped on my glasses. With the slightest bit of pressure, I switched them into night mode, allowing me to ascend the staircase at the end of the hall without resorting to lighting the gas lamps. I preferred not to make my presence known when I could help it.

On my first inspection of Sky Manor, I'd noticed a tower visible from the outside with no apparent internal access as far as I could ascertain. I needed to find a way to enter it, seeing as it was the most likely location for hiding the right key, assuming most of those I'd collected were useless. The vault, I assumed, would be someplace more obvious. Hiding things in plain sight suited the preposterous nature of this game.

I pulled back behind a bulky suit of armor at the sound of approaching footsteps. The set expression on Arden's face told me he was either considering looking for Jessie or had found a key. Either way, I wanted to put him on edge.

"Oh." Arden's face scrunched up in confusion at my sudden appearance. "It's you again." He reached up a hand, and I nearly thought he was going to try shaking mine, but instead he pushed his glasses farther up his nose. "Have you, uh, have you found anything yet? I know most everyone here, but it seems like there might be a few things Dad left out when he was helping me prepare." He raised an eyebrow, looking at me expectantly. He knew I'd been paid to protect him, but I could see the note I'd given him was causing him to question things.

When I didn't answer, he shrugged. "The game's starting to wear on me more than I'd expected." He cast a furtive glance over his shoulder like he expected the row of hollow knights to transform into automatons.

I tilted my head and arched an eyebrow, my lips curling just slightly on the left. It had been the look more than one man had glimpsed in his final moments. I clapped a hand on his shoulder and leaned in close enough for him to smell the mint on my breath. "I have some bad news for you, Ardie. You're on your own from here on out. I'd wish you good luck, but the lies are getting old." With that, I faded into the darkness and left him to his own devices.

Mister Woodhouse's Notes

Jessie—Main atrium—13 keys
Strategy: Brilliant slip of the hand.

Arden—Second floor passage—1 key
Strategy: Running his hand through his hair and sighing.
Should I tell him that will not make a key appear?

Benjamin—West stairwell—1 key
Strategy: Avoiding Camilla while trying to follow her

Camilla—Parlor—0 keys
Strategy: She's vexed! This is going to be a spectacle.

Rupert—Parlor—3 keys
Strategy: Meeting up with Camilla "secretly." Is this an
alliance or a tryst?

Maple—East stairwell—2 keys
Strategy: Marching through manor with shifty eyes

Zenith—Behind a coat of armor in the hallway—14 keys
Strategy: Putting everyone on edge. Again.

Vault-hidden

Chapter Ten

Arden, the Banker's Son

9:14 PM

I SNUCK DOWN THE staircase back to the bottom floor, each cautious step creaking and groaning like the rest of the manor as it floated through the clouds with its nonsensical pipes and gears. I wasn't fearful of the antique staircase cracking and sending me to my doom below the floorboards. No, falling didn't scare me, no matter how far I had to go. At least, it didn't a few hours ago. Now, I wasn't so sure. I huffed a breath through my nose and glanced over my shoulder, hopping the last few steps.

I had a crucial goal: a chance at a fresh, new life however short it might be. I couldn't let the drama of others—or any tangled feelings of my own—distract me.

So, why couldn't I shake the trembling in my chest ever since reading that note?

If I continue seeking the treasure, could it really cost the life of the sister I've given up on having? Could whoever wrote the note simply be stirring up old rumors to addle me? But no one knows how much I've longed for those whispers to be true . . . so out of all the tangible misdeeds they could have blackmailed me over, why did they choose that?

I rubbed my hands down my face, resting against the wall of the empty-yet-ever-gaudy hallway. So much for my plan of remaining apathetic. Mere hours remained to discover the vault and win my chance at changing everything. But if I truly had a sister, someone to care for beyond the world Father had carefully crafted me into . . . that nostalgic hope for connection seeped into my chest. As well as trepidation. If the note held truth and my success at this game was directly related to the life of my sister, it could only point to one answer: my sister must be in the castle too.

A shiver made its way through my extremities. The options of who it could be were limited. Camilla couldn't possibly be related to me. She had the nefarious, spoiled persona to belong to the Bentley name, but my father would never have kept the evidence of a scandal like an illegitimate child remain so intertwined with our family business. Someone in a lowly position like Maple's could make sense. But Maple was too sweet, too...innocent. No matter what possible secrets she could have, it would be a speck compared to my family's legacy. I wouldn't believe it, even if the note had directly named her.

Which leaves only the mysterious stranger who I couldn't trace any ties to when we all met at the zeppelin. Jessie. A thief, by the way the jewel-encrusted silverware appeared to disappear from the side of the table she walked around at dinner. Yet the way she easily invited me to search with her, the way she seemed she had something more to say before she was called away...*Does she already know?*

My head throbbed, and the buzzing feeling in my extremities wouldn't calm down—my medication must've been wearing off. *Didn't I take a swig of the new vial after Camilla passed it to me at dinner?* I could've sworn I did, between being pulled around by the others. Not that I would've let any of them see me take it and know I was at my weakest. Even Camilla didn't know what the continuous supply was for, assuming it to be for my father's usual misdeeds. *So perhaps I didn't take it?* My mind swirled with trying to remember.

I grasped the vial in my pocket, weighing it in my palm. More than anything, I likely needed proper rest. But there was no time for that. I slid myself up from where my back had slumped down the wall and took my hands from my eyes.

A metallic face caught my gaze from around the corner of the corridor's end. Nearly lifeless human-like eyes that made my skin crawl. As if I'd caught it where it shouldn't be, the automaton swiveled back in the direction it had peeked from. Not for the first time, I wondered if that weird Woodhouse might be dabbling in making the artificial beings more human than they should be.

Despite the internally screaming protest of my body, I made my feet move to the end of the hall where the automaton had disappeared. Where the corridor split into left and right, a bit of dewey green stuck out bright against the floor. I bent to pick it up and held it between my forefinger and thumb. A leaf, attached to a bit of vine. The first tiny hint I'd had to go on since that display of magical, creeping vines led me to a dead end at the conservatory before dinner. An automaton had carried a wilted plant away then, looking frantic to care for it. With no one else present at the manor besides Woodhouse, that would fall to the automatons, of course. Maybe the vines hadn't led me to a dead end at all. Perhaps they were leading me to the automatons. A grim smile overtook my face. *Why wouldn't the game lead me to dig deep and face my fears? Bravo, whimsical sky castle.*

I sighed and marched down the left fork, which led to a set of double doors. By the clanking and whirring behind them, I shouldn't have been surprised, but when I threw the doors open to the servants' quarters bustling with automaton chaos, I had to fight the instinct to turn and search elsewhere. Since robots didn't require much besides a charge, their quarters were devoid of any human commodities. Only a sea of emotionless faces lined up and crammed into the room from one end to the other. Sweat formed on my brow, automatons waking and swarming toward me as I entered the room further. Likely just ready to serve me as they were programmed for, but it didn't help my nerves. Their empty eyes caught mine, boring into my soul with their nothingness, as if they were ready to claim me as their sibling. I went from walking to sprinting toward the far end, until my foot found a cord.

In between the moment of going from upright to smashing to the floor, a cold hand grabbed my elbow and steadied me. I righted myself and turned to find myself standing with the same automaton I'd followed here. Its eerie green eyes took me in. Its fingers easily wrapped tighter around my arm, as flexible as my own hands despite its metallic nature. Reminding me of how much like them I was, so realistic and yet so programmed to do whatever someone else planned for me. I had to get out of there, and change that. I yanked my arm away and stepped backward.

Likewise, the automaton moved forward. I walked briskly toward the back of the room to try to casually explore like I'd come in there for, but I felt my new friend following at a distance, like a stretched out shadow. Breathing heavier, I reached a small door at a back corner of the quarters. *My escape.*

Not closed all the way, I flung it open and turned to find the automaton nearly close enough to bump into me. I stumbled backward into the threshold, and the door slammed closed.

Pitch darkness surrounded me in place of the pursuing dead eyes. I inhaled a deep, musty breath. It sank into my stomach, in a new sour feeling. No lights or sounds. It appeared I was in my own little box. I stretched my arms to the sides, and they both touched the cold stone wall, not extending all the way. This escape didn't lead to another room or a hallway as I'd hoped in my initial panic. Rather, it made a follow-up with my second-most fear: tight spaces.

More deep breaths. The wooden door of the tiny, closet-like space wouldn't budge. Whirring and clanking continued on the other side of the wall. I tested the ground with my shoe, only discovering some broken pieces of wood. *Breathe.* I held my head and turned around in the narrow space. *There must be something.* I reached overhead, unable to feel a ceiling, but a draft appeared to seep in from somewhere above. I patted along the walls some more. Stone. Stone. An entity with legs that I flipped away. Stone. Something thin and slightly damp. At first my fingers recoiled, but I forced myself to find it again and follow it farther. Almost like a smooth rope, making its way up and down the wall and tangling into . . . a clump of leaves.

A vine.

Heart beating faster, I took hold and gave the plant a firm tug. It didn't break. It had likely been growing here for decades. This chamber must have been some sort of servants' shortcut—a dumbwaiter, perhaps—before automatons dominated that job. With the smashed wood, perhaps some sort of bucket, possibly a way they took care of the latrine from the upper floors. Not something I preferred to focus on being trapped in, but if I was correct . . . it meant the vertical passage should lead to somewhere above.

Using a lower clump as a foothold, I hoisted myself up onto the wall. Feeling for and grabbing one vine at a time, I climbed upward into the abyss.

EVENTUALLY, THE DIN OF the bustling automatons faded to silence. After climbing what felt like the entire height of the manor, a crack of light became visible a few yards overhead. With a burst of elation, I grabbed vines quicker, the light ever closer. Finally at the reach of my fingertips, I lunged to the side and pushed the door. A figure darkened the opening, the likeness of my father's pinched expression peering down at me.

I gasped and nearly dropped my hold on the clumped vines.

The figure threw her arms out—too small to be Father—and worked to pull me through the square in the wall. Jessie and I picked ourselves up from the floor. I gasped in short breaths, unable to draw the oxygen I so desperately needed after that tight climb.

Two thoughts shifted back and forth. She looked just like Father with her forehead in worry. How did I not notice earlier? There was no denying our relation and the validity of the note. But secondly, any of the other competitors would've shoved the door and closed me in, a good riddance and better chance of finding the fortune themselves. Much more, if it sabotaged their estranged sibling who'd lived the lavish life they'd dreamed of while stealing silverware. *Why would she help me at all?*

I found my voice, but it came out quiet and vulnerable, not a quality I should ever show. "Do you know who I am?"

"I think most everyone knows who you are, Arden Bentley."

I had a hunch she knew that wasn't what I meant and waited for her to give a real answer.

She lowered her head, dark hair covering her face a little, but her words weren't as nervous as mine. "I have a feeling I don't need to tell you what I've been practicing and waiting to say. Long before I ever saw you on the zeppelin."

She's been wanting to talk to me, too?

I smiled a little. "You have Father's eyes."

"I'd always kinda hoped they were yours." She smiled back at me. "That it might be one connection I had to the brother I wished I could know."

Though I understood her sentiment, it still felt unreal, too easy.

"You . . . you don't hate me?" My voice wavered. "For having an easy life handed to me, for being forced into a job that everyone else despises me for?"

She shook her head. "I don't blame you. Until I see it for myself, I'd like to believe you're something more than the rumors."

That bursting warmth expanded in my chest. Someone was willing to see past who my life had made me into.

"I am more," I claimed with faltering confidence. "I-I want to be, anyway."

Jessie smiled. "Maybe we could be more together. If we get out of here. Supporting each other, as real family. Without thieving or lies." She looked down.

"I can't wait to get out of here then." I nodded, with the most honest, shaky smile.

A squeezing feeling gripped my chest. It was official: I had a sister. Someone to care for outside of the carefully placed associates my father surrounded me with.

"I'm sorry I couldn't be in your life before, but I hope I can make up for it now."

Jessie looked over her shoulder, as if she'd heard something. Worry crinkled her face. "As long as I've waited for this moment, it feels like there's not enough time."

I swallowed and nodded, the game still at stake outside our reunion. The only chance I thought I had to change things, slipping away with every tick of the clock . . . but maybe replaced by something even more valuable. "We'll meet again. No matter how things end or where the treasures end up."

Jessie fumbled with her hands. "Now that we've finally met, I hate to say goodbye. Maybe...could we search the manor together, and catch up on the way? I actually brought some things to show you, in case you didn't believe me. Pictures, letters. Would you want to see them?" She looks up at me in a pleading way I'd always imagined a little sister would.

I chuckle. *If she brought all that, she must have been waiting to meet me as long as I have waited to meet her. It's like the game doesn't matter to her anymore either.*

"Yes. I'd very much like to see them." I checked my pocket watch. The hands ticked toward 10:00. "I'll meet you back on this floor, half-after the hour."

"Until then, Arden." Jessie squeezed my hand before disappearing down the next passageway—leaving me standing in the hallway, starkly different from the me who'd been startled by thinking I'd seen my father's face just moments ago.

A few simple words ignited a sense of hope I never thought I'd hear from anyone else: *"I'd like to believe you're something more than the rumors."*

That phrase fostered my own belief that I could still become something besides the next generation of evil. If Jessie—the sister who could've easily spurned my entire existence—believed I was more, even before I could change my circumstances, maybe I didn't have to. Maybe I didn't need to buy my way out of my father's control, or take drastic measures to cut all the ties. What if I were to lose the game, but still find a way to walk away from it all without dirtying my hands further?

After tonight, I have a lot of plans to reconsider. Starting with my back-up plan with Ben.

Except my need for rest and air was increasing, despite this new light emotion and being freed from the automatons and the wall. My assigned bedroom was down the hall, but it didn't have what I needed—what I earlier noticed out my window. I crept to the room next to mine, and tried the handle. Unlocked, it pushed right open. Inside lay a bedroom with dark decor, and what I hoped to find on the far wall: doors leading to a balcony.

OUTSIDE, THE CHILLED, FOGGY night pricked my skin and refreshed my lungs though the sky's thin air didn't quite dull the dizziness. If I wanted to play the role of a worthy competitor and not push myself to bedrest, I had to do something. My only immediate option, I pulled the vial out by the chain and downed some of the sweet liquid. I braced myself with my hands on the balcony's walls, waiting for the healing poison to kick in and calm my symptoms. Wispy clouds gathered around the manor, masking its bottom layers and giving nothing away from this bird's eye view. Other than a curl of green swaying from the balcony's ledge, and cascading down the wall and into the mist. Another dreaded vine.

I huffed and tilted my head upward. *Funny, but no.* I wasn't climbing another wall in this condition. Besides, surely the vines didn't lead me all the way to the top of the manor just to lure me back down in a needless loop. Unless it had been a distraction of the manor's devices this whole time.

Giving the hanging vine one more consideration, I internally asked it to make things more simple—when a golden-bronzed glint shimmered in the revealed moonlight. *No. It can't be.*

I edged closer to the corner of the vine. The shimmer was definitely there. Something solid and not a trick of the lighting. Something key-like, wrapped up in an overgrown wad of foliage. My arm wouldn't fit between the balcony's decorative bars. But if I could hoist myself just far enough, I could grab the upper part of the vine and pull it up. I pushed myself onto my stomach, the wall edge nowhere near comfortable, and stretched for the vine. My fingertips just barely missed it with each swing of my hand. Bent over the railing, the rush of blood to my head pounded like rushed footsteps in my ears. Just one more try, and I'd attempt to concoct another plan. With all the energy I could muster, I swung at the vine. My fingers caught and gathered it into my palm.

In the same second I pulled, something pushed back. My feet left the balcony.

The vine in my hand snapped as gravity claimed my full weight. In the roaring rush of air surrounding my fall, only one thought pounded through my mind.

I'm sorry, Jessie.

Mister Woodhouse's Notes

Too busy cleaning up to check where everyone is...

Chapter Eleven

Jessie, the Thief

10:19 PM

I shouldn't let myself freefall with hope; the part of my brain where reason calculated the probability of Arden turning on me told me to stop indulging my desires, but I couldn't. Never in my wildest dreams had I imagined that he'd accept me as his sister. Once this was all finished, I'd have someone to call family. We could travel to the floating ruins together and tour the old abbeys where God had been worshiped for thousands of years. Even without winning this game, my life would take a sharp turn for the better . . . and I'd find a way to care for the orphans.

"Arden?" I pushed the door open to the bedroom where I'd left him so I could find the handful of portraits and notes now in my grasp, the ones I'd told him about.

The fancy room with its wood-framed bed and flowing curtains to a terrace remained empty like no one had used it. *Where is Arden?* A lamp flickered above a tidy desk with paper stacked into one shelf. The privy hadn't a sound coming from the dark closet. I closed the door and crept to the terrace doors.

The note I received earlier in the day screamed at me from my front pocket.

The clock ticks on your watch.

The children play hopscotch.

The key can't save them all,

So be sure to attend the ball.

There is one closer than a friend,

Whom you must apprehend.

My stomach plummeted with each step forward. *The note had been to scare me, hadn't it? Did the hopscotch have another meaning, or even the ball?*

"Arden, are you outside?" I tiptoed onto the stone terrace and panic fluttered in my chest.

Moonlight drizzled over my skin just as a cold breeze attempted to snatch the warmth within my soul. Goosebumps snaked over my arms and legs beneath the ridiculously thin gown I'd stolen from the Gold Digger.

Clouds reflected an orange-and-purple stream of soft light all along the seashore below, brighter than anything I had ever seen in the city. I leaned against the railing. The cold metal pressed into my waist, shorter than the ones I'd seen at the prep school back home. If a taller person leaned too far, they just might...

A shadow marred the terrace below.

A human figure sprawled on the stones, lifeless. My momentary awe disappeared. Dark liquid pooled around the figure and reflected the moonlight.

My heart dropped.

"Arden." The word escaped in a quiet plea. "No, no, this can't be." I checked the stones around the terrace for vines or a decent footing. In the dress I stole from Camilla, I didn't have a good enough chance to climb down and make it.

I had to get downstairs to the second-floor terrace. My mind whirred with ideas and short snippets of culprits. I raced out the room, nearly knocking into an automaton at the open door.

"How can I be of service?" the robotic voice asked.

I didn't stop moving to acknowledge the creepy thing. Feet pounding down the hallway, I tried to calculate the probability of Arden surviving a two story fall onto a stone floor. But I couldn't think past the image of him sprawled on the ground with blood around his head. Blasted moonlight didn't show the gravity of his injuries. Tears spilled down my cheeks as I turned into one of the fancy staircases with carpet running down the center. Spooky portraits stared at me from their high perches on the wall.

All of the painted eyes accuse me. It's your fault. You had to push the issue.

Pushed? Did someone do this to him or had Arden leapt to his own doom? Could it have been an accident? I had just seen him and he was fine.

My boots squished into the carpet, absorbing the thumping that would have thundered down the stairwell. I peeked out the third floor passage and Camilla's lean figure pushed into a bedroom. She hadn't seen me, so I rushed around the turn and continued my descent.

If Arden needed help, I had to get there sooner than later.

For all I knew, he could bleed out in the time I tarried. I skipped every other step until I landed on the second floor. I didn't bother with finding a door and opened a window to the communal terrace.

A creak cut through the space, and my training as a thief cringed inside. But I had to get to him.

I slipped through the narrow opening and sprinted across the stones to Arden.

His body remained like a black slash across sandstones. His glassy eyes stared heavenward, empty of soul. The congealed blood from his skull painted the grooves between the stones. I dropped beside his body, and blood soaked along the thin fabric of my skirt.

I grasped his icy hand. A chain with a tiny vial wrapped around his palm. A cold inhalation rushed between my teeth.

I unwound the chain and held it up to the moon. The half-empty bottle had to be the size of my pinky finger. It had chiseled glass designs and a golden cap connected to the linked gold necklace. I twisted off the cap and met a sweet aroma, too sweet. Poison.

Though some poisons could be medicinal in small amounts, they could also be deadly.

An ache pounded at the base of my head. *One person had to die for there to be a winner, but why did it have to be Arden? Did I inadvertently cause his death?*

Clutching the vial, I tucked it into a pocket at my waist. Dress pockets should become a norm, but it also gave me pause that Camilla would have sewn pockets and buttons beneath all her dresses. Camilla had passed something shiny to Arden at dinner.

If Arden hadn't taken too much poison himself or leaned too far off the ledge, it meant we had a murderer in our midst. In the games two decades back, the competition got so violent that the event was renamed Death Match in the newspapers. Almost a hundred people had shown up but half of them never returned because a handful of contestants had picked off the competition though only one death had been required.

I put my hand on Arden's fine jacket, hoping beyond hope that his chest would move. No such miracle.

Hot blobs of emotion streaked along my nose. "If anyone did this to you, I'm going to find them. If it was me, I'm so sorry. I had to tell you who I was. You are—were the only family I had." Heat swelled in my chest. He had been very alive before I left the room and had seemed excited.

God, if you are real, why did you allow this to happen? This wasn't an accident.

Swiping my cheeks, I couldn't contain the trembling and hurt clawing up my throat. "I guess this is goodbye."

A shroud of darkness covered me. What more was there to life? Even my orphanage would forget me if I never returned. I'd go into oblivion like a flower that bloomed in the spring heat and died in a day.

"I promise, if someone did this to you, I will find them." My fingers bit into my palms. "I will bring them to justice even if I have to do it myself."

Lifting my skirt enough to get to my boot, I fumbled across the various straps and compartments. One compartment at the heel held the lock-picking tools I planned to use at the vault. Another one held a slick gun, small enough to fit in a pocket.

I better get out of here before anyone accuses me.

I'd pay Camilla a visit to see what she had to say about this poison. Even a girl her size could make a man fall with the proper push.

I stood and contemplated my next move. Rupert would do anything for Camilla, though he wouldn't admit it aloud. I saw him pining after her, and since he'd already double-crossed me, I wouldn't put anything past him.

Zenith might be handsome, but he liked the shadows far too much.

Ben seemed like the type of person who'd kill for the key.

Maple had the innocent look of a dove, but she was here. Anyone who came up to Sky Manor had their reasons. Sometimes the sweet ones were the most poisonous of the bunch.

Stuffing the gun into my pocket, I slipped to another window and tested if it'd open. It lifted on a squeaky tread. Thieves wouldn't be an issue in a floating mansion. The irony mocked me.

I'd be the greatest thief of them all. Arden wouldn't die in vain.

Mister Woodhouse's Notes

Jessie—Main atrium—13 keys
Strategy: ???

Arden—Dead at the hands of a competitor

Benjamin—Unknown—1 key
Strategy: Perhaps stalking the cousin

Camilla—South parlor—0 key
Strategy: To ruin upholstery

Rupert—Unknown—3 keys
Strategy: Where did he sneak off to?

Maple—Approaching Terrace—2 keys
Strategy: ???

Zenith—Tower library—17 keys
Strategy: Reading up on Manor history (needs a distraction before he learns something he shouldn't. Thankfully, that's about to happen before he grabs that next book.)

Vault-hidden

CHAPTER TWELVE

Maple, the Nice Girl

11:03PM

MY SCREAM WHICH HAD felt like it belonged to someone else died on my lips. Blood. So much blood. Not Arden. Not Arden!

The sight of his sprawled limbs and wounded head brought a series of images into my vision, images I had wished to block from my memory forever. The last time I had given into my hate and let the darkness win, I'd lost control during a fight. And after, it was like I had woken up. The vision of blood could never be fully erased from my mind. I'd sworn off fighting ever since, all except the inner fight against the darkness. Until today.

I sank to my knees by his side and stared in horror at the broken body of my once-dear friend. I'd been so set on finding that prize, I'd briefly forgotten what it might cost. Did I cause this? Tears streamed down my cheeks.

Voices and footfalls reached my ears, breaking through the fog of confusion and grief overtaking me.

"Oh my." Woodhouse stood over me with a grim expression. "It never gets easier. I'm so sorry."

Seconds later, four of the contestants surrounded me and the body. A curse escaped Ben's lips at seeing Arden, and he turned away, his face turning sickly white.

"What happened here?" Rupert asked in a shaky voice, though his expression remained as dark as it had been when we'd spoken of Arden in the hall.

"Isn't it obvious?" Zenith answered in a far too casual tone. "*One must die.*' Somebody decided to speed the game along."

The night air grew thick with silence as we all watched one another with suspicion. I tried wiping my eyes with trembling hands, but my anger stirred when none of the others appeared the least bit broken up by Arden's death. I happened to know he'd been a friend or colleague to most of them. Rupert's earlier words echoed in my mind. *Arden Bentley is a friend to no one.*

"You're saying one of us is a murderer?" Ben broke the tense silence.

"Maybe not," Camilla spoke matter-of-factly. "Not everyone is here. Where's that— that" —she snapped her fingers— "Jessie girl. I swear I saw her running around in one of my dresses. If she was so brazen to take one right out of my luggage and wear it, what was to stop her from shoving Bentley to his death?"

Of course Camilla would accuse the easiest target. Jessie was like me: no connections, no money. The fact that Jessie wasn't present to defend herself was likely the only reason I wasn't the first name on Camilla's list of suspects. My growing rage which had fled the moment I'd found Arden began to rise again. Her callous words about his death and the half-smile she attempted to hide pushed me over the edge.

"It was you, wasn't it?" I accused as I rose from the ground, glaring at Camilla.

"*Excuse me?*" She stared at me like I'd grown a third eye.

"So quick to point fingers, while you silently gloat over his body." I spat out the words, which sounded so cruel, they felt foreign coming from my mouth. I didn't care. "What? Did your third romantic conquest reject your advances? Is that what drove you to kill?"

Camilla's face turned scarlet. "How dare you, you disgusting little rat! I bet you're just trying to cover up that *you* did it!"

Woodhouse needlessly came to my defense. "Maple seemed quite broken up about his death."

"Can't you all see she's putting on a show?" Camilla practically shrieked. "Everything this girl does is a performance. If anything, she's more shocked that there's a body at all. She probably meant to push him off this floating death trap. I would bet my entire wardrobe that under Maple's too-nice persona is a murderous beast."

"LIAR!" I screamed as I lunged toward her, my fury overruling my better judgment.

"Maple, don't." A strong hand landed on my shoulder from behind and instinct took over.

I spun, slamming a roundhouse kick squarely into the chest of my assailant. Too late to regret my actions, I watched Rupert's eyes widen on the impact before his body flew halfway across the terrace. His head hit the marble railing with a sickening crack, and his body fell limp.

Gasps rippled through our little group and all eyes turned toward me, reflecting my horror. Camilla's red face rapidly drained of all color.

Only one face didn't look so shocked, appearing almost amused.

"Well, I was wondering when you'd reveal your secret talent." Zenith smirked. "Anyone else doubting if this nice girl couldn't have easily knocked Arden from the balcony?"

I turned back toward Rupert's still form, as the weight of what I'd done tore into my soul. I choked on my words. "Is he dead?"

Woodhouse rushed to Rupert's side, placing two fingers against his pulse. I held my breath, waiting for Camilla's accusation to be proven true. I was nothing but a murderous beast.

"Just unconscious," Woodhouse declared. "Dear, dear, dear. He'll have a ghastly headache when he awakes."

Camilla's tense body visibly deflated. She shot me a lethal glare.

"You were right," I whispered. "I'm a monster."

I dashed past the shocked faces, escaping into the manor. I didn't know where to run. My room? They might lock me inside. Perhaps that was best. But if they believed me to be Arden's killer, they may try to enact justice. My body trembled as I stumbled through the halls, wondering where I could hide.

"Where do you think you're going?" Camilla's enraged voice trailed behind me.

Why did she follow? Didn't she see how dangerous I was?

"Stay away from me!" I called back as I frantically turned a corner. The halls began to feel like a maze. I had been down this one already, but it seemed longer somehow. I turned back and chose a different direction, then stumbled into a dead end. I spun to return, but Camilla blocked my way.

She pointed a gun at me. "You don't get to perform a stunt like that and then just disappear. You nearly killed him!"

"I didn't kill him," I croaked, raising my hands in surrender. Tears slipped down my cheeks. "At least, I don't think I did. I never would have wanted to hurt Arden."

Camilla cocked an eyebrow, barely lowering her weapon, but still keeping it aimed my direction. "I was talking about Rupert."

A sob escaped my throat. "I didn't mean to hurt him either. I just got carried away."

Camilla's face furrowed into a frown. "And what were you about to do to me?"

My mouth dropped open. *What had I been about to do? What had come over me?* I needed to get control again. "I don't know," I admitted. "You've always just been so cruel. I don't understand it. It makes me hate you."

Camilla lifted both brows at that. "Well, at least you're finally being honest for once."

I coughed through my tears. "Are you going to kill me?"

Camilla frowned. "I'm just trying to figure out what's actually going on here. Like, where did you learn to kick like that?"

I clenched my eyes shut before opening them again. "My father was The Woolfe."

Camilla stared at me, wide-eyed. So she recognized the name. Not everybody knew it, but many people still did, especially in the underground circles.

"He taught me everything he ever knew."

Camilla's hand which still clutched the gun began to tremble. "You've been taking my verbal attacks, and you're telling me that all this time you could have snuffed out my life without breaking a sweat."

I sighed and glanced away. But instead of answering, my eyes caught on a strange painting on the wall. A stone garden wall with a wooden door. But the keyhole beneath the doorknob didn't look merely painted on. I swore it appeared like an actual keyhole buried into the painting. And something glimmered behind it.

"What is that?" I asked, pointing.

"Nice try, but I'm not taking my eyes off you."

"No, just look." I kept my hands up in surrender and, still facing Camilla, took three cautious steps toward the painting. The barrel of her gun followed my steps until both I and the painting were in her line of sight together. "There's a real keyhole in the painting."

She squinted her eyes at the hole and it glimmered again. She took a sharp inhale. "Too bad we don't have a key."

But I did. The key I had found in my room. I hadn't given it much thought until after Arden had left me in the library. My stomach lurched as the memory of his last words to me entered my mind.

"Perhaps we can meet again, when this is all over."

I would never see him again. I held back a whimpering cry and reached into my pocket.

"Hey, I am *not* afraid to use this," Camilla shouted.

I pulled my hand from my pocket and held it out, palm open, for her to see. The key rested in my hand.

She stared at me like I was insane.

"Okay, well . . ." she paused as if trying to decide, then gestured the gun toward the keyhole. "Open it."

Slipping the key into the slot, I gave it a twist. The rumbling sound of grinding metal hit our ears and, without warning, the floor beneath us jerked into motion. The wall was turning, and part of the floor with it. I kept my balance, gripping the turned key as my anchor, but Camilla lost her footing and tripped, falling flat on her stomach.

BANG!

The gun went off and flew from her fingers, skidding across the rotating floor. I jumped and covered my ringing ears as I frantically looked over my body for a gaping wound I didn't feel. I appeared unscathed. Camilla scrambled across the floor toward her gun which had landed where the floor wasn't moving. But I watched as the walls completed their turn, and the final glimmer of light from the hall closed before even her hands could reach through. With a final slam, we were trapped in total darkness behind the walls.

Mister Woodhouse's Notes

Jessie—Lower level stairs—13 keys
Strategy: Not sure. Might need to enact automaton protection sequence

~~Arden~~

Benjamin—Outside Arden's room—1 key
Strategy: Trying to steal keys from the dead

Camilla—Hidden passages—0 key
Strategy: Round 2 of destruction

Rupert—Second floor terrace—3 keys
Strategy: Unconscious

Maple—North parlor—1 key
Strategy: screams, accusations, physical assault, and running away

Zenith—Second floor terrace—17 keys
Strategy: Appears to have altered strategy to become nursemaid to Rupert

Vault-Hidden

Chapter Thirteen

Jessie, the Thief

11:30 PM

BANG!

A distant gun fired above. I stepped off the last stair into the bowels of Sky Manor. My chest grew tight. Another person might be dead, and I hadn't a clue if we had one murderer or five.

Mister Woodhouse had to have answers.

But when I turned the corner into a cluttered workshop, I stilled. Shelves lined the walls and buzzing light bulbs hung over a large work table. Spare cogs piled atop every surface. I backstepped, but caught the sight of a door cracked open beside one of the shelves.

Should I go up to the main floor where competitors loomed and shot guns or get to the heart of this place?

Taking one steadying breath, I closed the distance to the back door.

Darkness encompassed a narrow stairway along with the hum of something beyond. Answers.

One last glance at the workshop assured me I was alone. I plunged into the darkness. My boots scuffed the floor—more noise than I would have liked. Yet, I'd risk capture. Mister Woodhouse didn't seem the fellow to exact extreme measures for justice. The farther down I went, the louder the buzz of mechanisms grew.

Was attending the game to meet my brother worth it? Was the possibility of winning the loot worth death? In the chilling passage bathed in shadow, I wasn't sure if the answer was yes anymore. The layers of voices from the orphanage's matrons echoed through my mind, telling me how God provided for me even in my poverty. *I should have learned better from them instead of chasing after the greed of what I didn't have. Now, I lost the one thing I actually wanted.*

Light drizzled onto the last steps, and I stopped to listen. The light bulbs buzzed, mechanics hummed, and a noise like a dim roar of fire drifted into my ears. At least there were no footfalls or the click of automatons strolling in the quarters. I peeked around the corner and caught sight of a door glowing along the edges.

Was that the heart of the manor? I'd heard rumors that each of these floating mansions had a living heart, but it seemed far-fetched. Now, I wasn't so sure.

I continued to take in the rest of the room's tan wallpaper, shelves with mechanisms, and brass inventions. I caught the back of Mister Woodhouse at a strange desk, tapping on buttons three yards to my right. The glass panels and moving pictures before him kept the old fellow from catching me spying on him, and my spot off to the side kept me from the reflective glass.

Though I'd seen many new inventions in the palaces of the wealthy who lived below, I had never seen something like this. My exhale pushed between my lips, letting out a wheeze in my awe.

Mister Woodhouse's head twisted a quarter, and I retreated into the stairwell. I'd have to return when no one else was here. I tiptoed faster than a rabbit eyeing a predator.

At the landing, an old automaton blocked my way. Its glowing eyes blazed with light as it scanned my body. I pushed past it and bumped the brass torso in my haste. I climbed the next set of stairs to the main floor, but clicking noises pursued.

A sleek automaton followed me down the long south passage at the clip of a newer model. It remained thirty yards away but would breach the space if I didn't change course. Its eyes focused on my every move, evident in the way its pupils grew and shrunk like the shutter of a camera. I couldn't seem to dodge it. I slunk into an empty library and closed the door.

Bound books lined three of the walls. Two windows framed a giant fireplace and several armchairs arched in front of the hearth. If I had any hope in finding a key to open the vault, I'd dive through those shelves.

What use was infinite gold coins if I died? Emotion clogged in my throat. I'd had a brother for not even an hour of my life, and I'd already lost him. My fists clenched.

The door opened. A robotic voice said, "Do you need anything, Miss..." It drawled the last word as if it meant for me to finish the sentence with my last name.

Investigating the rooms and luggage would continue to be an impossible feat with a constant companion. I'd have to go back and find Mr. Woodhouse to see what he could do about this robot. Even having it blocking my exit brought a shiver down my spine.

"I don't need anything. Now scram."

The automaton cocked its robotic head to the side as a hum of cogs churned.

"Don't bother. I'll leave." I sped through a narrow gap between the automaton and the door.

A brush of cold brass skimmed my wrist, but I ran around the corner and down a set of steps.

Even when I ducked and fled up a level, I heard the cogs churning from within the wood paneled walls. Thumping fists banged through the hallway like a thrumming heartbeat that had gone wild.

Faint screams rung in the passages as if the horrors of past competitions still lived in the corridors of the mansion, with all its papered walls and pipelined ceilings.

"Help me! Help us!" Female voices faintly screeched. "We're stuck."

I pressed my ear to a paneled wall. The voices murmured from somewhere within.

The clomp of robotic footfalls echoed in the stairwell, and I slipped into the closest doorway which turned out to be a pantry.

Shelves full of jars reflected dull light from the passageway. I crouched behind a large sack.

A mechanical whirr sounded through the open doorway as if the automaton scoured the mansion with one goal in mind.

Follow Jessie.

I held my breath, evading the possessed contraption.

Please skip the pantry. Please skip the pantry. How would I ever find my brother's murderer with this brass humanoid following me?

Mister Woodhouse's Notes

Jessie—Main atrium—13 keys
Strategy: Hiding in the pantry?

~~Arden~~

Benjamin—Main atrium—1 key
Strategy: Restarting from the beginning

Camilla—Hidden passages—0 keys
Strategy: Murder the nice girl, perhaps?

Rupert—Second floor terrace—3 keys
Strategy: Unconscious

Maple—Hidden passages—1 key
Strategy: opening hidden passages

Zenith—Second floor terrace—17 keys
Strategy: Still playing guard to Rupert

Vault-hidden

CHAPTER FOURTEEN

Maple, The Not-so-Nice Girl

11:45 PM

To my relief, the darkness did not last for long. After our screams died down, a whirring noise took their place. At first, I thought it was only the continued ringing in my ears from the gunshot, but then, as if by magic, a long row of gas lamps above us lit up on their own, one by one. The turning of the wall must have triggered some kind of mechanical system that lit a path which stretched through the long, eerie hall we'd now discovered hidden behind the mansion's walls.

"Are you going to kill me?" Camilla's whispered question echoed the one I'd asked her moments before. The hair on my neck stood on end, as I realized the terrible power I held now that she'd lost her weapon, and we were trapped together.

This awful place and this horrid game were both messing with my head, making it harder to control my thoughts. But the memories of Arden's death and what I did to Rupert sobered me.

I shook my head and spoke in a shaky voice. "I don't want to hurt anyone."

Camilla continued to stare at me, her face ashen. "I don't believe you."

Her words and tone caught me off guard. If she really thought I was about to kill her, I'd expect her to kick and scream, but she appeared to have accepted her presumed fate with quiet dignity.

I reached down a hand to help her from the ground and she flinched. I searched for words that might put her at ease. "If I wanted you dead, Camilla, you would be." Morbid as I felt saying the words, it was the honest truth.

Camilla shoved my proffered hand aside and blew out with her lips. "And why not? I've known all this time that you had to be hiding something sinister. But I never expected to watch you slam Rupert across the terrace like that." Her voice caught.

"How can you say you didn't want to hurt anyone, when you nearly robbed him of his life?"

The terrible image from the terrace returned and I backed away from her, my limbs numbing. Why did she care? I remembered Rupert's sad story, and accusations flung from my lips. "As if you cared about him at all. I might have broken his body, but you didn't hesitate to break his heart in order to go after a richer man. His cousin, no less."

As soon as the words left my mouth, I knew I'd said the wrong thing. White rage flooded her cheeks. But rather than shooting more insults or accusations like I'd expect, she stood coolly with an arrogant smirk, dusted off her gown and turned toward the dimly lit hall.

"Since you claim you don't plan to kill me, I'm going to find a way out of here." She stepped past me with sure and confident steps.

I realized she planned to leave me in these secluded halls. Alone.

I glanced at shadows that lurked in the tall ceiling above the low-hanging gas lamps. While their light had been a relief, they weren't exactly bright. I shuddered, dreading the nightmares of my past that haunted me anytime I found myself alone in the dark.

Though Camilla was the last contestant I would have wanted to be trapped here with, I still preferred her smug company over the monster within me.

I chased after her. "Wait, I'm coming with you."

She didn't answer, but a subtle tension relaxed from her shoulders. Interesting. Maybe I'd succeeded in convincing her I didn't plan to kill her, or maybe she dreaded being lost and alone in this place as much as I did. She pressed forward in silence.

This hall seemed endless. My heart thumped within me as we continued down the corridor. It almost appeared to be growing narrower, but maybe it was my paranoid mind playing tricks on me.

I kept trying to find something else to say, something to put us both at ease, but every time I opened my mouth, the words died on my lips. She didn't want to hear any cheery anecdotes from me after my cruel remarks.

"I never wanted to hurt Rupert." Camilla spoke so softly, I almost didn't catch the words. "I didn't even want to leave him. But I had nothing. I did the only thing I knew to do, in order to survive."

She said nothing else, and my steps faltered. For a brief moment, she sounded so broken. It was the least heartless thing I'd ever heard from her mouth. Was she allowing me a glimpse into the real girl under all her glamorous pretense?

As I hurried to keep up with her, a wave of guilt washed over me. Who was I to accuse her of pretense? If anyone understood what it felt like for desperation to lead one down paths they'd come to regret, I did.

Maybe it was finally time somebody else knew about my dark secrets.

Mister Woodhouse's Notes

Jessie—Main atrium—14 keys
Strategy: Not sure. Ate a few figs.

~~Arden~~

Benjamin—Back outside Camilla's room—1 key
Strategy: Has this fellow ever played a game before?

Camilla—Hidden passages—0 keys
Strategy: ???

Rupert—Second floor terrace—3 keys
Strategy: Still out cold

Maple—Hidden passages—1 key
Strategy: survive

Zenith—Second floor terrace—18 keys
Strategy: Gathering keys while he waits for Rupert to awaken

Vault-Hidden

Chapter Fifteen

Camilla, the Gold Digger

12:01 AM

THE SILENCE BETWEEN THE supposed nice girl and I would have been welcome if we hadn't been trapped behind a secret wall and if she hadn't just struck me in the heart. I did love Rupert. I did.

How could Nice Girl understand the impossible choice I'd had to make? The tip-tap of our shoes pronounced every one of our movements. We still had eight hours before we'd be stuck here for a year. A year for Rupert to find a prettier girl, one who hadn't traded him for his cousin. One who didn't need extra funds to feed her family something besides beans.

Maple mumbled.

"What? What do you want?" I spun around, forgetting she could knock me down with a single strike.

Her eyebrows furrowed in contemplation. "I shouldn't have said that about you and Rupert."

"No, you meant what you said. Stick with it. I don't like all the pleasantries, and I can say we are firmly past that sort of relationship."

"We've passed so many doors and portraits, and this passage doesn't seem to end. Shouldn't we try a door?" She reached for a handle. The practicality of her statement deflated my puffed up temperament.

I took a steadying breath. We'd need each other to get out of here. I reached for a door handle. "Fine. We'll do things your way. Since I'm a complete mess of a person and a failure, we'll follow your lead."

"That's not what I said." Maple pressed her fingers to her forehead.

"Then what did you say? I'm certain it wasn't that you admired my affinity for poison or that you admired my better attributes."

"Poison?" Her bottom lip quivered, and her hand went to her slender neck. "Did you mur–"

"Not on purpose." I turned the handle.

An empty room with green wallpaper stretched before us. A single armchair sat in a corner.

Maple's eyes sprang wide open, and she flinched her head back. Her expression matched my sentiment.

"It's not here." I slammed the door shut and strode to the next door.

"Camilla, did you poison Arden?" Her question didn't hold an accusation but rather a soft touch.

I twisted the handle and pushed open the next door. Red wallpaper spread across my vision. One gaslit lamp stretched its arm from a wall and cast orange light over the room. Instead of an armchair, an automaton twisted its head in my direction. The click-click of its cogs churned as it spun around with a knife in its clamp. I slammed the door shut.

"Run." I didn't wait for Maple to respond. My heels clomped on the hardwood as we stomped across the dark, narrow passage to who knew what.

"Camilla, Camilla, what are we . . . running . . . from?" she asked between gasps.

"Killer automaton." I glanced backward but the passage behind Maple was empty. I stopped.

Maple stopped with me and slapped her hands on her knees. She inhaled and exhaled deeply. "Killer automaton?"

"It had a knife." A chill slithered up my spine. The stale air in this secret place threatened to suffocate us. Even if I didn't get the money, we had to get out of here.

"Are you sure?"

I could have strangled her with my glare.

She lifted her hands in a motion of surrender. "Do you think he died from your poison?"

Hot tears sprang to my lashes. Something cracked inside of me at her gentle question, yet I couldn't let myself be broken. "It's not like you're perfect." I swiped at my eyes and continued to a portrait on a wall. There could be a key or a hint in it somewhere. Opening the rooms didn't seem like a good option anymore.

"You're right." Maple sidled up next to me, her voice low and gentle. "I killed someone."

My heart dropped. My goodness. I was stuck in a passage with a real murderer. Trying to keep myself from trembling, I swallowed hard.

"It was my last fight, I needed the coin. The bets were high, and the darkness overtook me. It's like I got so caught up in the fight and the cheers that I didn't stop." She cried.

What was I to do? I'd seen people hug others at times like this, but it didn't seem appropriate to coddle her for beating someone to a pulp. Yet again, she might be able to say the same about me, and she hadn't.

Maple sniffled and wiped her nose with her sleeve. "But I didn't kill Arden, I'm sure of it now. In fact, I believe . . . I loved him."

I cringed but tried to keep my face still. Who could love someone like Arden? A thought crawled into my gut and wove a tight web. With the way I had treated Maple, she might wonder who could love Camilla.

Maple continued, "I thought that he might have felt something, too. But I see now how foolish I was. He didn't even remember my name."

Though she had stopped crying, the pain etched on her pretty face tightened my chest. I wanted to stop her tears when an unbidden memory appeared. "Well, if I recall correctly, he did know your name."

"You don't have to make up some story to try to make me feel better." Maple lifted the corners of her mouth, showing off the reason I'd nicknamed her Gigglemug.

"No, really." I turned toward the portrait on the wall again, unable to meet her gaze. "He defended you when I made . . . a remark."

She chuckled. "I've made one or two about you before. I'm not the nice girl everyone thinks I am."

"Perhaps—" I twisted my mouth, unable to work around the hot lump in my throat—"that's why we're both locked away in here?" I stared at the portrait of a lady so far removed from this moment, yet staring at us in accusation.

Maple looped her arm through mine as if we had settled into being friends. "Is it worth it?"

"Being trapped in here? No."

"The money?" she asked.

Cogs whirred from somewhere back where we'd come from. Nerves twisted in my gut.

"I really did see an automaton with a knife." I pulled her along, walking deeper into the neverending passage. We had to find a way out before the end of this game and before we both wound up as corpses.

Mister Woodhouse's Notes

Jessie—Second floor room—15 keys
Strategy: She might be spying. The figs awakened her spirit.

~~**Arden**~~

Benjamin—Kitchen—1 key
Strategy: Maybe eating an apple with help, the poor boy

Camilla—Hidden passages—0 keys
Strategy: Surviving

Rupert—Second floor terrace—3 keys
Strategy: I should probably go and check on him again. . . .

Maple—Hidden passages—1 key
Strategy: staying close to Camilla

Zenith—Second floor terrace—19 keys
Strategy: Finding keys I forgot were even there

Vault-Hidden

Chapter Sixteen

Rupert, the Poor Scoundrel

12:20 AM

The world was spinning. I groaned, one hand going to the back of my head where I'd collided with the marble. My vision began to clear, but the pain only worsened. *Where did Maple learn to do that?* How *did she do that?*

My eyes swept around. *Wasn't everyone here just a moment ago?* Perhaps I'd hit my head harder than I thought, but I'd been sure everyone had been here. Now, only the strange fellow who'd introduced himself as Zenith remained, his expression pensive. The dim light from the nearby torches cast ominous shadows across his face, pale against his dark clothing.

"Where . . . ?"

"Maple ran out in tears as soon as she realized what she'd done. Camilla went out shortly after," he said. He pulled me to my feet. I noted that he hadn't bothered explaining where my wretched cousin had wandered off to. Not that I cared.

I slowly nodded, but then my gaze caught on something to my right.

Right. The body. My pounding skull had made it easy to forget Arden Bentley's body, broken on the floor. A chilling reminder of just how dangerous this game had become.

The image of Camilla passing something to Arden under the table rose up in my mind, darkening my thoughts. *Could she have—*

I bit down hard on my tongue, telling myself to stop jumping to conclusions. I'd never even confirmed that Camilla had given Arden poison. I could be completely wrong.

But the thought provided little comfort; as much as I didn't want to believe her capable of such a thing, once the idea had sprung up, it had spread through my mind like a cancer, too deadly to dismiss.

I cast a subtle glance at Zenith, wondering if he'd had any part in all this. I knew next to nothing about him, and none of the other competitors seemed to either, Arden included. Meaning he had no personal reason to kill him.

Not that you need one in a game like this.

"So, what were you doing before the body was found?" he asked. His eyes, narrow and probing, made me feel like an insect under a magnifying glass—all too seen. And all too helpless.

"I was just . . ." My mind struggled to come up with a reasonable excuse. I could hardly admit where I'd really been. I didn't want to go to prison, especially after I'd been so careful about staying aboveboard for the past two years. "I was searching for keys, of course. Wasn't everyone?" I raised my chin a bit. "Not that it's any of your business."

Zenith raised an eyebrow. "Unless you're the murderer."

"I—" Sweat ran down the back of my neck, my veins throbbing with a heavy dose of adrenaline. I quickly excused myself and headed to the washroom. The lights in the room made my headache even worse. I splashed some water on my face, scolding myself for getting so worked up. I'd known things were going to get unpleasant. I'd known that when I'd agreed to this horrible game.

But knowing it would eventually happen and peering into Arden Bentley's dead eyes were two very different things.

I heaved into the sink a few times, losing the food I'd eaten at dinner. *That was, what? Several hours ago now?*

I hadn't even thought to check the time. I reached for my pocket watch, only then remembering I'd left it in my room. It had to be sometime after midnight by now. I'd been here for over nine hours, and I was still no closer to finding the vault than I had been when I'd first arrived.

I shook my head. *What does the treasure matter anymore?* All the money in the world wasn't worth it if I never got the chance to use it. I'd rather live poor than die like Arden had.

My thoughts strayed to the blackmail note I'd received. Whoever had written it had known about my past as a smuggler, a past I'd too easily turned back to when I'd thought Camilla needed my help.

Perhaps she still did. After Jessie had refused to help me steal the vial from Arden's room, I'd gone searching there myself. But I'd found no sign of it inside. I'd been about to leave when the door to the room beside me had creaked open.

Was Arden in there? And someone else, too? Two sets of footsteps had entered, but only one had left. I'd stayed hidden, waiting for whomever was still there to leave.

Then Maple's scream had changed everything.

What if Camilla changed her mind and tried to get the poison back, but Arden refused? Or, what if he decided he no longer wished to be "business partners" and tried to kill her, only for her to push him to his death first?

Or—I gulped, not wanting to consider this possibility—*did Camilla double-cross her so-called "partner," tricking him into thinking he had a tonic when it was poison all along?* If that was the case, he could have fallen from the balcony once the poison had taken effect.

I had to get to the bottom of this. I stalked through the mansion, not bothering to greet the automatons I passed. I was on a mission that couldn't afford to wait.

It may not have been Arden and the killer in the next room when I'd been snooping, but that seemed like the best place to look. Perhaps a clue had been left behind. Or perhaps—if Camilla was the killer—she'd come back to make sure she'd covered her tracks.

When I reached the room, a petite figure was stretched out over the balcony, preciously close to falling.

I shot forward without thinking. "What are you doing?"

The girl wobbled, nearly slipping over the edge, but I grabbed her around the waist and pulled her back.

But the person I'd rescued wasn't Camilla Carranza. It was Jessie.

"You nearly sent me to my death!" Her anger quickly dissolved, and she stepped away from me, fear dancing in her gaze. "Or was that your intent all along?"

Her arms were stiff against her body, her hands clenched into fists.

"What? Jessie, do you seriously think I could do something like that?" Our partnership hadn't ended on good terms, but I would have thought she knew me better than that. I'd always been staunchly against violence.

The suspicion in her eyes was answer enough. "If not that, then what are you doing here?"

I crossed my arms over my chest. *Fine.* If she was going to act like that, I wasn't about to tell her the truth. "I came because I was looking for the key."

She scoffed and spun away. "Look." She pointed to the courtyard. Right to the spot where Arden Bentley's body had lain a few minutes ago. The automatons must have removed it, but a few bloodstains had been left behind. "This must be where he fell from."

"Why do you care where he fell from? I thought you were after the treasure."

"Things have changed."

I frowned. From what I remembered of our time working together, she'd always been single-minded about her goals. Very good at reaching them, too. But those goals had always had to do with the next hit, not with justice. In fact, when I'd told her I was done with that life, she'd mocked me, told me there was no use in following the law when it was already so broken.

Or perhaps the reason she wants to uncover Arden's killer is more personal.

I opened my mouth, wanting to ask more, then stopped myself. That wasn't important right now. "Did you find anything that might explain who killed him?"

Jessie whipped around. "Killed him? How do you know someone killed him?"

"I—I just assumed . . . I mean, what other reason would there be for him to fall?"

Guilt flashed on her face for a brief second before she tucked it away, her eyes hard. "None. There's none. And no, I haven't found anything."

Her tone sounded sincere, but Jessie had always been an excellent liar.

I nodded once. "Then, have you seen Camilla?"

She rolled her eyes, then replied, "She and Maple left together after Maple knocked you out. I haven't seen them in a while."

Her story lined up with Zenith's, except now that I thought about it, I didn't recall her being there when the rest of us had gathered around Arden's body. "So, you were watching when we found him." It wasn't a question.

"*I* found him," she corrected, her voice strangely choked. As if he'd meant something to her.

"Were the two of you . . . ?" I trailed off, hoping my insinuation wouldn't come across as insensitive. In all the interactions I'd witnessed, they hadn't seemed to know each other. *Then again, appearances can be deceiving.*

She shook her head, a sheen glinting in her green eyes. "I better go." She slipped out of the room, leaving me to wonder what their relationship might have been for her to be so shaken. In all the time I'd known her, she'd never been one for attachments. Jessie was all business. Or had been.

My gaze swept over the room, wondering what Arden could have been doing in here. *This is Zenith's bedroom, isn't it? Did the two of them meet, argue perhaps, and then Zenith pushed Arden to his death?*

The idea seemed plausible. It would certainly be a relief to know Camilla hadn't been involved. *But what about the vial?*

I searched the room much as I had my own, checking everywhere a vial might have been concealed. When I rifled through Zenith's bag, I came across a very familiar seal among his papers. I pulled out the blackmail note, just to be sure.

It was exactly the same, which meant he was the one who knew my secrets. *Does that also make him the killer?* I needed to find more evidence, something more concrete, if I was going to make any accusations, so I continued my search.

When my fingers grazed the back of a rather ugly bust on the mantel, pain shot through my index finger. I pulled my hand back, but then something clicked. A panel in the wall just above my head shifted, revealing a small compartment. *Just like Maple said . . .*

I reached my hand inside, feeling around the edges until I grasped something cold. *A key!*

It was a simple golden skeleton key, without any filigree or symbols. I clutched the metal to my chest. *Is it even worth hunting for the treasure now? Should I just focus on clearing Camilla's name?*

How did Zenith not find this? It hadn't been very difficult. As I turned the key over in my hand, a drop of blood welled up on my index finger. An idea began to form in my mind. . . *Perhaps Zenith already searched the bust, but it needed* my *blood to unlock its secrets.*

But why? Is this some sort of test? The only way for me to win is by going back to my old smuggling ways?

I sucked my teeth, cursing Sky Manor for its manipulation. And myself for falling for it.

I took another look at the key as I cradled it in my palm. So small. So innocuous. I pulled the other three out of my pocket, then flung them all across the room. I wouldn't play this game any longer.

Mister Woodhouse's Notes

Jessie—Tailing Zenith—15 keys
Strategy: Not sure but it's entertaining

~~*Arden*~~

Benjamin—His bedroom—1 key
Strategy: Feeling sorry for himself

Camilla—Hidden passages—0 keys
Strategy: Surviving

Rupert—Zenith's bedroom—0 keys
Strategy: Awake again, disposed of his keys. Seems exasperated. Possibly due to concussion?

Maple—Hidden passages—1 key
Strategy: following Camilla

Zenith—Main library—20 keys
Strategy: Refusing to let Jessie know that he knows she's there

Vault-Hidden

Chapter Seventeen

Camilla, the Gold Digger

1:30 AM

Locked in the magical passages with Maple, I determined two things:

1. I'd never want to get in a physical confrontation with her.

2. The vault's riches would never solve the deep heartache beneath my breastbone.

It almost made me regret what I'd done to Arden. I pushed that sentiment aside, feeling the telltale prick of tears irritate the back of my eyelids. We had also lost the one key we'd found. Real tears did threaten to fall.

Maple continued to stride ahead through the dark corridors lit by the occasional sconce in this space that defied reality. Every door either led to a room that did not exist on a map or to another passage. Shiny pipes and curly vines overhead acted like they had some place to go and some job to do. If I could figure out their purpose, that would possibly help. We'd get this lost-in-a-maze thing over with.

"What are you going to do when you get out?" Maple asked, looking over her shoulder.

A snarky response wanted to leap off my tongue, the part of me that was still frustrated at the possibility that we might never be free of this place. I heaved a sigh. "I don't know."

"I'll quit fighting if you quit poisoning." Her voice was sickly-sweet, like the smell of nightshade.

"You push too hard. I still need to earn a living." I gestured to a door to our right and raised a questioning eyebrow.

She stopped in front of the door, blocking my exit with a severe maple-colored gaze that matched her name. "Then promise me you'll at least break it off with . . . what name did we give your boyfriend?"

"Ben."

"I was going to say the peacock." She laughed to herself.

Though I wanted to join her, I couldn't. She would have given me the same label as him a couple hours ago. And Ben had his own troubles and heartbreak that I couldn't ignore. He'd grown up without worrying about his next meal, but he'd never had the affection I'd received growing up. His upbringing wasn't his fault. Yet . . . I'd overheard a conversation. One that left a single word echoing through my mind.

Disowned.

What depths would he sink to—no, traverse—to maintain his wealth? Would he dive as far as I'd already gone to gain riches?

"Camilla? Camilla? I didn't mean . . ."

"Yes, you did."

A beat passed, and she didn't try to amend her statement again. We continued through the darkened passage with unspoken tension between us, though my previous distaste had been smothered by a heavy helping of panic.

Would I be arrested for Arden's death? Murder was still murder even in this silly game.

Arden had been the worst sort of person, one who had known too many of my secrets. I'd be a prime suspect if they ever found the bottle I gave him.

Though Ben drove me mad with rage, I couldn't believe he had killed Arden. The only one I could imagine killing him other than me was Zenith. That Jessie girl was rather odd, so perhaps she could have, too. I'd be safe enough from accusation if we could ever get out of here.

"Camilla, didn't the pilot say that we had to be at the zeppelin by morning or else they'd leave us here?" Maple's voice quivered with the fear I couldn't voice.

I turned in her direction. Behind Maple, gold flecks of light gathered to form the shapes of two young ladies. Beside a portrait of an old man with a pipe hanging out his mouth, the ladies pushed open a secret panel.

"Do you see that?" I pointed toward the apparition.

She swung her head around just as the flecks of light disappeared into a dark crack in the wall. The sliver of darkness closed again, intact.

Maple's bottom lip quivered. "Do you think?"

"Let's go through it."

"But the last time we followed its lead, we got stuck in here."

"And now I don't hate you."

The slash of her mouth broke into a grin. "Does that make us friends?"

My muscles slackened. I had plenty of friends at the apartments back home and plenty of people who had pretended to be friends at school. Though I didn't need another person who expected something from me, I couldn't deny her what she longed to hear. "Friends, but on the condition that you let me slowly quit poisoning on my terms and that you accompany me when I cut ties with Ben."

"Done."

I felt my lips curl but slid the mask I liked to wear quickly back into place. We couldn't allow sentiment to get in the way of returning to reality.

In a silence much more amicable than the last one, we strode to the portrait, inspecting the grooves on the metallic frame. Maple dragged her fingers over the cherry wood behind the portrait. Though all appeared normal, the sensation of the painting's eyes following me ticked up my heart rate.

Maple punched the portrait, leaving a hole in the canvas, and drew back her fist, shaking out her hand.

"What was that?" I asked.

"You didn't see the way he was ogling you?"

"I'm not too sure your outburst did us any favors either."

"It was creepy."

"I can put up with creepy if it means we're free."

She dragged her fingers along the curvy edges, but then we spotted a strange round shape connected to a long edge with jagged grooves. I reached for the key, but Maple's hand bumped mine out of the way.

Heat flared in my cheeks. I rocked forward on my toes, ready to pounce on her. Maple gave a gleeful look, the type of joy a six-year-old girl expounded—wait, was the word exuded—well, *showed* when she received a new doll. I couldn't fight her, so I'd have to play my cards right.

"Do you think it is *the* key?" I asked, resisting the urge to snatch it from her.

She twirled the four-inch piece between her fingers, inspecting the winged designs and grooves that had hid it so nicely in the portrait frame. "I don't know."

"We'll open it together?"

She stilled for a beat and settled into her gigglemug. "Of course. We found it together."

My lips twisted up into what I hoped was a genuine smile.

A whistle of air wheezed in front of us. The wall parted with enough room for one person to squeeze through the dark gash ahead.

Grabbing Maple's wrist, I stepped into darkness, keeping one arm out, so I wouldn't guide us into a stone wall.

Maple stumbled behind, but I couldn't let the passageway shut her out while she had the key and leave us both alone in a labyrinth. Sky Manor had its own mind, and I wasn't sure I trusted it. A grinding noise cut behind us, and the manor shut us in complete darkness.

"I really don't like the dark," Maple whispered.

"We're going to get out." I plunged ahead, stepping forward, forcing myself to continue in spite of the abyss all around.

A fever climbed my neck. We weren't dead yet, and as far as I could tell, hours hadn't passed since I last saw a clock. We hadn't missed the zeppelin. If we had to claw our way out of this fortress, we would do it with my heels.

"I really, truly, don't like the dark."

"We're almost out." My nails dug into her skin, trying to keep her from being left behind. That key might not be my salvation, but it would be something for the both of us.

"What if we die here and we end up two skeletons in a dark passage for the next year's crazy game?"

"Stop panicking." I plunged ahead into the void. When Maple grunted, I barked, "Do something useful. Pray, I don't know."

"All right. Dear God, I don't want to die. I don't want to end up as dry bones after having done nothing good in my life."

My annoyance shot like a pistol. "You do know prayer doesn't have to be so loud?"

"It's just—the dark. And death. And I just wanted to find the vault. I don't want to die."

Taking a steadying breath, I resisted the urge to scream at her for vocalizing the terror already consuming my insides. No, I hadn't done anything worthwhile in my life either. If we ever got out again, I'd confront Ben. I'd tell Rupert what I'd done and how I felt about him. Would I still fulfill orders when I got home? The inky black air seemed to press in like claws, showing me a future where a judge would send me to the pits for the death and destruction I had caused.

I wanted to lash out at God for making me poor. Yet, even with no gold coins or soft materials atop my dry bones, I had life, family, and hope of winning this thing. In this grave, there was nothing. The only one to call on was God, the one who kept this island from crashing into the ocean.

"Yes, I give up," I whispered to myself. "I will stop poisoning. I'll make things right."

A small sliver of light cut into my vision, and I clicked forward. My heels tip-tapped faster. "Maple, do you see that?"

"See what?"

My legs flew me forward.

Maple inhaled. "Oh, sorry, I had my eyes closed. I see it now."

When I arrived at the light, I met a crunch of leaves in a gap in the wall about two handbreadths thick. I didn't wait for Maple's approval to push through. Blessed dappled light pierced through the windows into a room with a single fireplace. Vines hung all up and down the sides of the mantle.

On the other side of the room, a giant dark metal door with a metal lock and keyhole stood in a wall between the bookshelves as if it was an everyday piece of furniture. *Is this the answer to our prayers?* I needed to pray more often, but I wanted a more genuine one like Maple's prayer.

"Do you think?" Maple opened her hand, the golden key in her palm.

"Let's try."

She squealed with delight and skipped ahead of me. "Come on, Camilla, you have to turn the key with me. I don't know how it works. Is it the person who turns the key or the first one in the vault?"

I blinked warm tears from my eyes, too overjoyed to say a word. Maple lined the key up in front of the keyhole. I placed my hand over hers and we jammed the key into the blessed hole.

But we couldn't turn it.

Maple continued to use her bulging muscles, sweat trickling from her hairline. My heart dropped into my stomach and cooked like gizzards in boiling water.

All of this for nothing.

Mister Woodhouse's Notes

Jessie—Tailing Ben—16 keys
Strategy: What is she doing?

~~**Arden**~~

Benjamin—His bedroom—1 key
Strategy: Still pouting

Camilla—Vault room—1 key
Strategy: Alliance. I didn't expect that.

Rupert—Main library—0 keys
Strategy: Wandering from room to room. Looking for Camilla?

Maple—Vault room—2 keys
Strategy: Alliance

Zenith—Dining room—21 keys
Strategy: Studying the cutlery, as though he needs any more blades on his person

Vault-Revealed

Chapter Eighteen

Ben, The Emerald Prince

Exactly 2:00 AM

Air.

I needed air.

This whole floating monstrosity of a manor was getting to me. There was no way off and nowhere to escape. These people were all insane. Even Camilla was acting different. She was never this brazen—this *reckless*. She was going to ruin everything . . .

if I ever found her, that was. I hadn't seen her in a few hours, and honestly, it was helping my suffocation a little bit.

A cog churned slowly somewhere above my bed before a pipe belched out a steady stream of white steam. I watched as it unfurled and billowed across the ceiling, momentarily covering the obnoxious mural. All too soon, the steam dissipated and I could once again see emerald paisley set against a gold back. White stags jumped and stretched, looking more like disfigured hares than Cervidae.

It matched the gaudy gold bed frame and emerald duvet perfectly, and I hated it. I didn't know what kind of magic this place had, but having my room match my family colors was a sick joke I just couldn't forgive. It only reminded me of how much I desperately needed to find the fortune.

I won't lie, after a few hours, Arden's idea to erase my debt became more appealing. All I had to do was go over, ask for a loan, get rejected, and make sure I slipped a glove off before his father shook my hand. No one would ever know—and if they did manage to find out somehow—it would be easy to frame Camilla.

With a sigh, I sat up and swung my legs over to the floor. I hadn't bothered to take off my shoes before lying down, but my jacket hung off the back of the nearby wooden chair. My worn, white gloves were folded neatly on the corner of the desk by my jacket. I balled my fists momentarily before relaxing them. I stared down at my palms as the sting of poison surged and bubbled up to my fingertips. I still wasn't completely sure how my power worked, and neither was Camilla, but I knew that the oily black poison beneath my skin reflected my anxiety perfectly.

Groaning, I dropped my hands and stood. There was no use moping about it any longer. I needed to find a key, and fast. I knew there were several already floating around, but each time I figured out where one was, it was already gone. It was like this house hated me. I ran a hand through my hair and picked up my jacket. I shrugged into it and snatched up my gloves.

A heavy *thunk* sounded as something landed on the floor. Swearing under my breath, I bent down to pick up whatever it was. Cool metal brushed against my fingertips, startling me momentarily. I wrapped my hand around it and stood.

I knew what it was before I opened my hand. The teeth stuck out past my thumb, and gemstones cut into the fleshy part of my palm. Slowly, I unfurled my fingers. A blood-red copper key, perfect in every way, rested in my bare hand. It was heavier than I expected, and slicker than what I was used to without the glove. Little bumps and ridges bubbled along the neck, making it appear like it had only been poured a few hours ago. As smooth as it was, its texture was nothing like I'd experienced.

Three teeth poked out of the top. Two long prongs flanked one half their size. They were evenly spaced and had what looked like little spades at their tips. The gemstones were immaculately placed at the other end. A large emerald cut into an oblong octagon sat in between two circular sapphires. Two thin rows of diamonds surrounded each stone, and I knew that this key alone would be enough to cover my many debts.

Camilla would have loved it, but I would die before letting her see it.

An uneasy feeling washed over me, telling me to stay in my room. To stay and keep the key for myself. I wouldn't need the fortune, just the key. But if there was a chance that this key was the right one, how much greater was the reward inside the vault? A voice that sounded a lot like my mother's reminded me that too much greed always caught up with you. I gripped the key hard enough to hurt as I shoved the voice away.

No.

There was a reason this key was in *my* room.

It was meant for me; so was the fortune.

I slid the key into my pocket next to Arden's blackmail note. The paper had only gotten heavier since his body had been found. I honestly couldn't believe it—*still* couldn't believe it. He was just lying there for everyone to see. It wasn't right.

I shook the images from my mind as I slid my gloves on. I had a key, so there was only one thing to do now. I wasn't sure where the vault was, but the automatons did. I thought back to my conversation with Woodword—or was it house-something?—earlier. He'd mentioned where the ports were, and now I could comb through the recordings to find the vault. And while I was there, it wouldn't hurt to destroy any other implicating evidence there might be as well.

Making sure my gloves were snug, my hair wasn't mussed, and the key was in place, I left my room.

I hurried down the hall, and as I did, I thought I heard a crash and a faint scream that sounded a bit like Camilla. I whipped around, but only steam seeped out of one of the pipes. This place was a mess. If I hadn't known better, I'd say there were lions living in the radiators and parrots screaming in the pipes. Cogs clashed and clattered as I continued on, whirling their displeasure at keeping the manor afloat.

Frankly, I didn't blame them.

It took me a few wrong turns to find the stairs that led down to the first floor, then a few more to find the door to the servants' quarters. The old oak door didn't match the rest of the Manor. Where everything was bright colors, plant life, and brass, this door was simple and unassuming. The iron knob was rusted along the rim. I hesitated, trying to remember where I last saw the butler.

If the handle was rusted, and he was the only one here, that meant he spent a lot of time opening this door. I couldn't do what needed to be done if he was down there—or if anyone else was around. Pulling out my pocket watch, I checked the time. There was a little less than two hours left of the competition. I didn't have time to wait and think—I needed to get down there now.

I snapped the watch closed and ran my thumb over the emerald owl out of habit before stowing it away in my breast pocket. It was now or never. Taking a deep breath, I grabbed the knob and twisted. The door opened easier than I anticipated and I smashed it into the wall. The echo ricocheted off the wall and down the stone steps. My breath hitched as all the air in my lungs caught. I slowly closed my eyes and waited for someone to come running down the hall or up the stairs.

When no one came, I opened my eyes and released my breath. My palms grew damp inside my gloves. What I wouldn't give to take them off, but I couldn't risk accidentally touching someone. It happened once when I was young with a servant. I can still remember the way my father shouted in the hall as my mother gave me my first pair of gloves. They were custom made—emerald with our house crest branded into the backs.

I made to flip on the light switch, but then I noticed an electric bulb buzzing next to the door. It sat in a sconce and acted as an electric torch. I grabbed it, making sure it had a switch in case I ran into trouble and needed dark, then stepped down onto the stairs. I gingerly shut the door so it didn't make a sound, and continued down.

The stone steps were steeper than I'd anticipated. With a shaking hand, I reached out and groped for a rail. I didn't dare take my eyes off the stairs. When my hand caught only air, I felt instead for the wall. The chill seeped through my glove, reminding me of my sweaty palms. Not only that, but sweat gathered at the back of my neck now as well.

My labored breathing filled the area, and I tried to remind myself to calm down. I started counting the steps to distract myself, but a bang like a gunshot sounded below me. I jumped as my heart lodged in my throat. My left heel slipped, and I landed on the stone, *hard*. My teeth clacked together painfully, and I slid all the way to the bottom of the steps. I panted, trying to catch my breath and calm my rapid heartbeat at the same time. Darkness surrounded me, and it was only then that I realized I'd dropped the light somewhere on the stairs.

I leaned my head back on the bottom step. I didn't know what I was going to do short of crawling up the stairs on all fours. I winced, remembering the broken bulb on the stairs. One or both of my hands would never survive the trek. I swore again, then stifled a shout of surprise as acid-green lights flickered to life in the darkness. Long runners covered the stone hallways, and the sickly glow shone from under them. I crawled to the nearest one and lifted the corner of the rug. A symbol greeted me, and I recognized it from school. I'd seen it before—in a textbook about radiation.

I dropped the rug as if it were contaminated and scrambled to my feet. I checked to make sure I still had the key and hurried down the hall. I didn't know exactly where I was going, but the butler had said the room was under the kitchen and dining room. That was left, so I would probably run across the room sooner or later.

I passed several doors, and each one had some sort of noise coming out of them. I thought I heard a monkey behind one, and when I passed another, the gun went off again. This time though, it sounded more like a blown gasket. To convince myself it wasn't some sort of specter, I cracked the door open. A glowing automobile sat with an open hood as a mecha poured that same glowing green liquid into it. The machine turned its head slowly, and I shut the door before it could see me.

I moved on, growing more anxious the longer it took to find the automaton workshop. I started opening all the doors I passed, not wanting to risk missing it. All I found were empty rooms that would have housed living servants. They'd all been turned into mini laboratories and each held some sort of half-finished experiment. I remembered reading about a doctor who turned himself into a beast in the newspaper, and I was suddenly more afraid of the butler than I had been since meeting him.

As I neared the end of the hall, a door caught my attention. It wasn't like the other oak ones that I'd barreled through like some deranged bull. Instead, the dark mahogany gleamed in the sickly green glow. I stepped closer, and could make out a brass cog where the doorknob should have been. A whirring sound, like that of a fan, could be heard on the other side of it. The butler had mentioned something about keeping the mechas cool to prevent from overheating. I paused only long enough to check my pocket watch, using the light of the radioactive glow below me. The second hand had just passed twelve, making it five minutes to 3:00.

I swung the door open and ran bodily into someone. They dropped something that clattered to the floor. Snatching it up, the person stood, and I could make out the strong jaw and dark eyes of the guy trying to pass himself off as a teenager. My eyes dropped to his hands and widened in horror. They clasped onto a disk of film. I took a hurried step back and hit the wall. I met his dark eyes, and he smirked. I wasn't sure what he'd seen, but he knew something. Fear squeezed my heart, and I did the only thing I could think of.

I ran.

Mister Woodhouse's Notes

Jessie—Tailing Zenith again—18 keys
Strategy: Starting a key collection

~~Arden~~

Benjamin—Unknown—2 keys
Strategy: Running around the basement

Camilla—Vault room—1 key
Strategy: Jamming the vault lock with the way she's stuffing the keyhole with Maple's keys

Rupert—Kitchen—0 keys
Strategy: Watching the automatons to make sure they're not putting anything strange in the food.

Maple—Vault room—2 keys
Strategy: Letting Camilla use her keys

Zenith—Somewhere he shouldn't be—23 keys
Strategy: Sleuthing. And putting on a show of not noticing Jessie behind him

Vault—Revealed

Chapter Nineteen

Zenith, The Assassin

3:30

I KILLED HIM. I killed him. I killed Arden.

I might not have been the one who literally pushed him over the edge, but I killed him all the same.

I can't even begin to remember the first dead body I ever saw. Even my fondest childhood memories of my mother are surrounded in blood. Being an assassin was the only logical outcome of my upbringing. I have followed orders, I have killed with various methods, and I have walked away unscathed. But something about seeing Arden's broken body hit me in a way none of the others ever had.

Maybe it was because I knew him. He wasn't a void behind a marked face. Maybe it was guilt, tied to the wad of money his father had handed me to keep him safe. Whatever the reason, from the moment I saw his body on the ground, I swore to find the killer and exact what justice I could.

The slender metal disk in my hand was sure to hold the answers. I'd been so intent on collecting it, I'd nearly allowed that arrogant idiot to sneak up on me. But now, alone in my room, the time had come to see just who was innocent and who had pushed Arden to his untimely death.

I scrubbed the oil from my skin before I could begin my perusal. The cursed automaton had not willingly handed over the disk to me, even though I'd input the proper code. I'd worked through the code cipher from Woodhouse multiple times to be certain it was correct. But when I'd typed the numbers on the hidden keypad on the back of its neck, the blank metal face of the automaton had shifted, a spark of something glittering in its glass eyes. As though it knew something it was unwilling to share. So, I'd been forced to disembody the thing in order to free the mechanism and retrieve the evidence I needed to discover the culprit.

I cursed my shaking hands as I slotted the disk into the contraption I'd purchased for viewing the film. I slipped on the special glasses and watched as scenes from the day flashed across my vision at high speed. The bot had been busy, its comings and goings often unnoticed by the players, giving it access to more information than I'd expected, including capturing me slipping notes to my oblivious opponents. As the scene of me informing Arden he was on his own flitted past, I considered corrupting the file, but restrained myself from being too hasty. There was sure to be something incriminating someone else, so I kept watching.

THIRTY MINUTES AFTER I began my study of the film, the rattling of my door knob snapped my attention back to the present. I stashed the glasses under my pillow and straightened my jacket before opening the door. A particularly austere automaton tilted its head up and to the side to make it appear as though it was looking me in the eyes. "The ball is about to begin." It nodded twice, then turned and proceeded down the hall.

I'd had experience with mechs in the past, but these creations of Woodhouse put me on edge, especially after everything I'd witnessed on the film.

I checked my timepiece. The ball was slated to begin in fifteen minutes, giving me just enough time to finish watching the disk. The scene fluttered back to life, and my pulse quickened. All the secrets and lies played out before me. I held my breath as Arden climbed onto the ledge, balancing precariously to reach into the shadows of a twisting vine. And then, the moment of truth.

With a controlled expression and erect posture, I tapped the wall in the sitting room twice as I'd seen a pair of automatons do on the film. The muffled voices on the other side silenced as the panel slipped away. I quickly surveyed the scene as both girls shifted to hide something behind them. So, they'd found the vault, but judging by their rumpled appearances and slumped shoulders, whatever keys they might have in their possession were not the right key.

Maple's face brightened, and it looked like she might try to hug Camilla. Apparently their hours in the back passages had proven to be a bonding experience.

"Evening, ladies." My voice betrayed no emotion. I extended my left arm to Camilla and my right to Maple. I would wait to share my revelations with the entire group. It was enough to leave the two of them uncertain as to how I had discovered them in this hidden room. "Might I escort you to the ball?"

Camilla quickly shifted her expression of shocked relief to flirtation. "I've never been one to turn down a handsome gentleman."

My skin crawled as I made sure to keep some distance from the vials clinking in the folds of her skirt. Most would believe the sound came from the bracelets on her wrist, but I was all too aware of what she carried and the damage they could do if improperly handled. She adjusted her skirts, undoubtedly wishing she had time to change before appearing at a formal event. A smug smile turned the corner of my lips when I glimpsed a smudge of dirt on her cheek and noticed her limping slightly after traipsing around all evening in her miserable high heels.

"Thank you for finding us," Maple gushed as she took my proffered arm. "We were beginning to worry we might be swallowed by this dreadful mansion forever." Despite her best attempts to look demure and innocent, I could feel the strength in her hands.

We traversed the passages to the ballroom in silence, Camilla doing her best to hide her limp. An automaton in a ridiculous French maid's cap stood beside the door. When we reached the entryway, it swung the door open, raised its hand to its mouth, and made a trumpeting sound.

"Introducing Zenith Laurus and the ladies Camilla Carranza and Maple Hill." The girls both gave little curtsies, and I released their arms, allowing them to glide into the room on their own.

Taking a moment, I took in each of the other players in the room. Ben stood off to my left, a glass of brown liquid in one gloved hand and suspicion in his eyes. After he'd run away from me earlier, I'd wondered if he would show up at all, but there he was, his other hand hidden inside the pocket of his obnoxious green suit coat. Camilla made her way to his side, strutting as though the hem of her skirt wasn't torn and dusty, head held high despite the dark streak across her cheek. She paused briefly, casting a contemptuous glare at Jessie, who looked absolutely radiant in her pilfered gown. Camilla lifted the skirt of her soiled gown in clenched fists. Her hiss to Ben was just loud enough for me to make out the words. "She stole my dress. Who does she think she is?"

Ben had the good sense to roll his eyes only after Camilla had glanced back to the state of the disgraced gown she was wearing. "I don't understand why we even have to be at this ridiculous ball." She raised her voice enough for everyone to hear her contempt as she yanked off her high heels. "I want to go home. The vault is a farce."

Maple kept glancing at Camilla, even as she moved to stand closer to Jessie. I observed the pair and noted that, despite the way the elegant gown accentuated Jessie's figure and made her hair shine, the little thief looked defeated. Her shoulders slumped, and her sharp eyes were paler and softer than I'd ever seen them.

The automaton trumped again. "Introducing Rupert Nelson." I shifted my attention quickly to Rupert. His eyes honed in on Camilla first, as though she were his magnetic north, even when she had clearly swapped poles. He ground his teeth at the sight of her swaying beside his cousin and practically stomped across the floor to stand beside Jessie and Maple.

I cleared my throat, and all eyes turned to me. Nerves, confusion, and terror rippled through my audience. *Good. Let them be afraid.*

I pulled the disk from my pocket, and someone gasped. It didn't matter who. There was enough guilt in the room to make even the mildest player want to keep their secrets hidden. I lifted the disk higher, letting it catch the light.

"You've all been very busy these past few hours. I have to hand it to you, I never expected so much cunning or cleverness from the lot of you, but you managed to give me quite a show."

A pair of automatons dressed in matching fedoras and bow ties wound between the players, carrying platters of long-stemmed glasses filled with sparkly liquid of every color under the sun. I paused to let the competitors select their beverages.

A show is always better with a drink in hand. I selected a vibrant turquoise liquid, emptied it before the bot had a chance to remove the platter, then selected a second drink, this one fuchsia.

"In case you're unfamiliar with film disks, I was able to record your activities with the help of one of our mechanical friends."

"This is preposterous." Ben set down his drink hard enough to crack the base. It was a good thing for him that the emerald liquid was a precise match for his pompous evening attire. "You've been spying on us?" Ben scoffed dramatically to cover his blunder in showing emotion. "Why should we trust the words of someone who doesn't even play by the rules of the game? Speaking of which, perhaps it's time for you to come out and tell us all just how old you really are."

Unperturbed by his outburst, my eyes flitted back to Jessie. She took a step back, as though considering making a run for it. As if the dress on her back wasn't enough to confirm her thieving ways. I could scarcely contain a chuckle, considering how clearly she had managed to outshine Camilla in her stolen dress.

"*Tsk, tsk.*" I cast Ben a contemptuous glare. "I think you've said plenty already this evening. And you won't want to miss what I have to say."

Ben downed the rest of his drink in one gulp before whisking a fresh drink from a platter and shifting closer to Camilla.

"As I was saying, I came here with a decent amount of information concerning each of you, but what I have viewed here"—I waved the disk again—"is even more priceless than those secrets you've been so desperate to keep."

"Oh, just get on with it." Camilla tossed her dark locks and slipped a hand surreptitiously into the pocket she wanted to keep hidden in her long skirt.

"I suppose honesty is the best way to deal with liars. There's some truth to what Ben said. I'm not one of you. I was hired by Mr. Bentley to keep an eye on Arden and give him an advantage. He'd done a healthy amount of research on each one of you ahead of time"—I leveled them each with a stare—"and I put it all to good use." I pulled out my favorite quill pen with a smile and noticed how pale Maple had become. Jessie shook her head and sighed. "The one thing he failed to research was his choice of assassin."

"I knew it." Ben pointed a gloved finger at me, the first time he'd released the thing tucked in his pocket. "I knew I'd seen you before. You did a job for my father once. You're way too old to be here. You must be, what? Twenty-seven? Thirty?"

"Yes, yes. An irrelevant detail at this point." I shook my head. "What really matters is the evidence on this disk."

I turned first to Rupert. "You might wonder why I was there when you awoke after our innocent little prize fighter almost did you in. I had a theory that you might have pushed Arden to assure you would get the prize so you could finally prove your financial value to Camilla." Rupert's cheeks darkened, and he spun to watch what Camilla would do. Her cheeks flared as well, confirming my suspicion that, despite her flirtatious ways, she did genuinely care for him. "But it didn't take long for me to realize you were horrified by the body. Not because you had doomed him, but because you simply don't have the stomach to kill."

"Unlike you."

I ignored Ben's side comment and moved on to Maple. "Your little stunt very nearly made you a murderess this evening. But while you have the power to take a life, your past actions have shown that you're no murderer. Even the man you nearly ended in the ring lived to tell about it, and I'm aware that you've not returned to the fighting circuit since that incident."

"It might as well have been murder, considering how I ruined his life," Maple muttered, her self-deprecation barely audible.

I gave her a nod of acknowledgment, well aware of the fine line between committing a crime and living a life dictated by circumstances. "You really should get that temper of yours in check, though," I added for good measure. "Perhaps Miss Camilla has a tonic she could give you to keep things under control." I didn't miss the way Camilla's arm whitened as she gripped the vial concealed in her pocket. "Speaking of which, would you mind telling me exactly what was in the vial you slipped to Arden?"

Camilla's face blanched until she was nearly as white as Maple. "It's just a tonic, like you said." A puff of air escaped from her lips, almost a giggle, as she waved the vial in the air as if to prove its innocence along with her own.

"Of course." I nodded. "Which would be the reason Arden started hallucinating after he mistakenly took it when he thought he was taking his medication." I paused just long enough for them to digest my words. "He was dying anyway, you know? By the color of his skin and the way his hands were shaking over dinner, it's likely his time was limited. But ingesting poison . . . "

"I didn't poison Arden." Camilla's drink sloshed citrine liquid on the floor as she waved her hands in protest. "He bought that from me."

Ben shifted away from Camilla, and she flew at him. "You can't let him accuse me of this."

Unruffled by her display, Ben did little more than narrow his eyes even more in my direction.

"You're right, of course." I gave her a placating nod. "And he never would have made the error if he hadn't been distracted by his conversation with Maple over here. You and your peach scones." I shook my head, and the girl turned nearly as green as the pale drink she carried. "It seems he remembered you, after all. He made his mistake shortly after your exchange. I took the liberty of checking the vials he had in his luggage, and the coloring is almost identical. So, when he was feeling dizzy after talking to you, he felt the vial from Camilla in his pocket and took a swallow, believing it was going to soothe his symptoms. It wasn't a large enough dose to kill him"— Camilla sighed audibly— "but the effects did have a serious impact on his thinking.

"Which is why, when he leaned out the window and saw something shining in the vines, he thought he'd found a key. By his actions, it was clear his vision was blurring and his movements were unsteady."

"Sounds like he did it to himself." Ben smirked. "He took the wrong medicine, got all confused, and just fell."

"Oh, but there's more." My gaze flicked to Jessie. "I was very curious about what he might have been reaching for. It seemed odd that Sky Manor would deliberately lure a player to death. Not very sportsmanlike. And when I reviewed the film I discovered the 'key' he was trying to reach was not one of the house set." It was Jessie's turn to fade to a spectral shade.

"I . . . I . . ." She gasped the words as if she were drowning.

"Naturally, you couldn't have known he would be the one to go after one of your decoys." I shook my head, genuinely feeling sorry for the girl. We had more in common than she realized. "But there he was, reaching out, thinking he might finally have a chance to make his own fortune."

The two automatons had continued circling with their platters throughout my speech, and they now came to stand on either side of me, as though reveling in the reveal as much as I was.

"In the end, I hate to admit the truth." I shrugged, and the others leaned forward. I looked at the automatons flanking me. "These bots have no feeling. They wander this place, doing what they have been built to do. They feel no pity when a player dies and would have no qualms about filling our glasses with poison. I have been like them for many years, going from job to job, taking lives as directed. I'm not proud of it, but I won't make excuses for myself. And for the first time, I failed my job. I killed Arden."

Glass shattered as more than one of the group dropped their glasses on the floor, speckling the marble tiles in a kaleidoscope of colors.

"He confessed." Ben's glee echoed through the vast ballroom. "You all heard him."

"Yes." I lifted my head and looked him straight in the eyes. "I didn't protect Arden, so there was no one to save him when *you* pushed him."

Mister Woodhouse's Notes

Jessie—Grand hall—20 keys
Strategy: Reselling keys for silvers? Using metal to make her own coins?

~~**Arden**~~

Benjamin—Grand hall—2 keys
Strategy: What strategy? Everything just blew up in his face.

Camilla—Grand hall—0 keys
Strategy: Surviving

Rupert—Grand hall—0 keys
Strategy: Surviving

Maple—Grand hall—2 keys
Strategy: Surviving

Zenith—Grand hall—23 keys
Strategy: Throwing everyone off-kilter

Vault-Revealed

Chapter Twenty

Rupert, the Former Smuggler

3:46 AM

THE WORDS WERE BARELY out of Zenith's mouth before my coward of a cousin shoved Camilla into Maple and tore from the room. Maple tried to catch Camilla, but she lost her footing, and the two girls tumbled to the floor with a loud thud.

"He's not getting away that easily," Jessie snapped, bolting after Ben as savagely as a panther chasing its prey.

Zenith's enigmatic "hmm" was his only response. Having said his piece, he seemed strangely content to just watch how the events unfolded.

"Are you all right?" I asked, helping Camilla to her feet.

She rubbed her forehead but nodded. "We have to help her."

"Yes, let's." Maple cracked her knuckles, the motion sending a tremor through my body as I recalled how easily she'd propelled me into the railing earlier. She lifted her skirt in one hand, then rushed out of the room.

Camilla and I moved to follow, but Zenith said, "No need to rush." He took a sip of his sparkling beverage, a slight smirk on his face.

"Rupert, let's go," Camilla urged, her hand still in mine.

My face warmed. I knew I should let go—she was still technically Ben's girl, even if he was a murderer—but her fingers just fit too perfectly with mine. *I've missed her so much—*

A cry outside made the two of us jump, and Camilla dropped my hand.

"Ben?" Her eyes widened.

The door swung open and in came Jessie and Maple, followed by two automatons holding a struggling Ben by the arms. His face was swollen, and a trickle of blood stained his mouth, but my cousin was a fighter; I'd give him that.

Maple locked eyes with him, and I had to hold back a chuckle when he dropped his head in defeat. The blood on her fist made it pretty obvious where his injuries had come from.

"Where would you like us to put him?" one automaton asked, directing the question to Zenith.

I frowned. *Since when have the automatons started taking orders from a contestant?*

"The zeppelin will be back to pick us up in"—Zenith glanced at his wristwatch—"half an hour or so. Lock him in his room until then."

"Half an hour?" Camilla cocked her head to the side. "I thought the game ended at 8:00."

The right side of Zenith's mouth tugged upward. "That's only if you're following the rules."

"In that case, we'll all be out of here soon. Before that happens, though, I want to know why you did it," Jessie snarled at Ben, arms folded over her chest.

My cousin's wry laugh made the hair on the back of my neck stand up. "Wouldn't you like to know."

"It's obvious," Maple piped up. "He's a cold-blooded killer who only cares about money. Arden just got in his way."

"It probably had something to do with his gambling problem." Camilla put a hand on her hip and glared at her boyfriend. "Did you owe him money?"

When Ben didn't respond, Jessie lurched forward like she was about to attack him.

"That's enough," I shouted.

The girl swung around in confusion, as did the rest of the guests. Part of me knew I shouldn't be surprised—I was hardly the most commanding figure in the room—but it still rubbed me the wrong way that they expected so little of me.

"But he killed my brother," Jessie said.

What?

Maple gasped, one hand covering her mouth. "Your brother?"

The rest of the group seemed just as shocked as she was, save for Zenith, whose cool arrogance was starting to get on my nerves.

I studied Jessie's features more closely, trying to find any sort of resemblance between her and Arden, but I came up empty. She wasn't the sort to make up something like this though. If she said they were siblings, it must be so.

"He deserves far worse," she added, then nodded at Maple. "Think you could hit him a few more times?"

My heart went out to her, but I couldn't let this continue. Not when there were better ways. "He does deserve worse but not like this. Let the authorities take care of him."

"But he—"

"Don't use Maple to let out your anger."

"She's not the only one who's angry," Maple said. "Arden—he . . . he meant a lot to me." The girl's voice cracked as she finished. Tears shone in her eyes, but she blinked them back, her gaze turning cold as it strayed back to Ben. "You aren't even sorry for what you did. Well, I'll make you sorry!"

Her fist connected with his jaw in a sickening crack.

"Maple, remember your promise," Camilla said.

Maple's arm, still raised, began to tremble. She glanced at her tight fist in horror, then at Ben's bloody face. She slowly lowered her hand, but it continued shaking at her side.

"This manor brings out the worst in us, myself included," I said with a sigh.

The terrible thought I'd had when I'd cast aside the key from Zenith's room returned, this time with a deep resolve that chased away my fear. "And it's time someone did something about it."

I turned and marched out of the ballroom, my head held high.

"Rupert, wait," called a sweet voice.

I whirled around, my heart catching at the sight of Camilla running toward me. She grabbed my hands. "Where are you going?"

Could it be . . . Was it not all fake? Does she have real feelings for me? The look of worry on her beautiful face seemed sincere, but that was impossible. She'd only been with me for my money; that was why she'd left as soon as it was gone.

I gently pulled my hands from hers. "Shouldn't you be with your *boyfriend* right now?" I couldn't keep the bitterness from my tone.

She winced, then glanced back at the ballroom door. She shook her head and returned her gaze to me. "What I *should* be doing and what I want are two different things." She put her hands on her hips, her voice growing sharper. "Now, I know you're up to something. What are you hiding from me?"

Hope sparked in my chest. *She does care for me, doesn't she? Maybe not as much as I do for her, but at the very least, she's concerned about my well-being.*

"You want to know what I'm hiding?"

She nodded, the motion sudden and impatient.

I hesitated. If I told her my plan, she'd surely try to stop me, and I couldn't have that. I had to tell her something though.

In the depths of her beautiful brown eyes, the answer came to me all at once. *If I'm about to die, why bother pretending anymore?*

"The truth is, I only came here for you."

Her brow furrowed. "Rupert, what do you mean? You couldn't have known I would be here. I . . . I stole my invitation, actually."

I shook my head. "No, I mean, I thought if I won the game, you would come back to me. That's why I agreed to this awful game in the first place." I let out a harsh laugh. "But I see now that this is too dangerous to continue. It has to be stopped, once and for all."

Fear flickered across her face. "What are you going to do?"

I leaped forward and pressed my lips to hers, the touch sending warmth skittering through my body. Enough to bolster me for what I was about to do.

I pulled back, wondering what she was thinking. But all I could see in her expression was shock. I swept my finger down her cheek, then tucked a loose strand of hair behind her ear. "Don't wait for me."

Live the best life you can, and forget about me, I wanted to say, but I kept those words tucked away in my heart.

I placed one more kiss on her forehead, then darted off, ignoring her calls to stop. I'd seen a green glow on the floors earlier, telling me of the radiation just below my feet. While it might be powering Sky Manor now, it could also be used to destroy it.

It took some time, but I finally found the source of the radiation on the basement floor: the automaton workshop. I gingerly stepped inside, knowing the automatons would try to stop me if they discovered my purpose. But failure wasn't an option at this point.

Various mechanical body parts sat in rows at the back wall, ready to be put to use when needed. A mechanical arm sat in the center of the room beside a long table covered in test tubes, notes, and beakers. A series of pipes ran along the ceiling, clanging and whistling every few seconds. Off to one side of the room was a huge tank full of bubbling green liquid.

Is that the source of Sky Manor's power? The tank had several tubes jutting out of it that disappeared into the walls. I wandered over to it, stretching out my hand—

"Can I help you, sir?" Woodhouse asked.

Where did he come from?

The man glanced from me to the tank and back, his eyes full of suspicion.

"I just need . . . to . . ."

"There's nothing in this room that will help you with the competition, I'm afraid. Best you head on out." He placed a hand on my back and guided me toward the door.

I didn't fight him—not until the last moment, at least, when I shoved him out and locked the door behind him.

"Mr. Nelson, sir!" He banged on the door. "Sir, open the door!"

"Get out of here while you still can, Mr. Woodhouse. The zeppelin should be here by now."

The banging stopped, followed by a soft, "Don't do this, sir."

But it was too late to change course now.

I grabbed a handful of beakers, each sparkling with colorful liquid. I had no idea what they contained. I just hoped combining them would prove dangerous enough. I raced over to the gleaming tank, yanked off the top, and tossed the beakers inside.

When the liquid began to roil so much the entire tank shook, I knew I had succeeded.

The pipes above me started bursting, crashing to the floor in pieces. I ducked, then charged out, the temperature in the room already unbearable.

I was glad when I didn't find Woodhouse waiting on the other side of the door. If he was smart, he was already headed for the zeppelin. I prayed he'd have enough time to make it.

I doubt I'll be so lucky.

A wave of heat hit my back as something exploded, then everything went dark.

Searing pain in my shoulder and a scream were the first things I was aware of as I came to. I coughed a few times, my lungs full of smoke as I tried to figure out where I was. The floor felt solid enough. *Am I still in the hall?*

"Get up, Rupert. We have to go," cried a voice nearby.

I squinted through the smoke, just barely able to make out a figure in front of me. My shoulder jerked forward as the person tried to pull me to my feet.

"Camilla?" I stood, then fell against the wall when the floor rumbled beneath us. "You came for me?"

"Of course I did, you fool. I love you. Now, get up, or do I need to go get Maple to make you?" A bloody cut lined her right cheek, and her dress was torn in several places, but to me, she'd never looked more perfect.

"But I told you to—"

"You can thank me for not listening *after* we get out of here," she snapped, tugging me forward again.

We stumbled through the hallway as more explosions roared in our ears, our hands intertwined. Flames licked the floor, devouring the manor with an insatiable hunger. Smoke was everywhere, forcing us to move by memory rather than sight.

"Come on," I coughed, tugging Camilla along when she faltered.

My head was still a bit dazed, but I was almost certain I'd told Woodhouse to escape on the zeppelin. There was no way it would still be there by the time we arrived—if we arrived at all.

Once we were outside, it became clear it wasn't just Sky Manor falling apart. The entire island was shaking like it was about to plummet into the sea.

"There!" Camilla pointed toward the end of the path we were on.

My eyes bulged at the impossible sight before me, but my legs propelled us forward even faster. Either I was losing my mind or the zeppelin hadn't left yet.

When we got close to it, Jessie opened the door and leaned out. "Hurry up, or none of us are getting out alive."

I didn't need to be told twice. Once Camilla had gotten inside, I followed after her, taking a seat at her side. The others all looked at us in relief, all except Ben, who sat gagged, bound, and perfect hair mussed in the corner. His eyes narrowed when he spotted us, but whatever insult he tried to share was muffled by the cloth around his mouth.

"Captain, we're ready," Zenith said, still as calm as ever.

Soon, we were airborne, and the island was just a burning speck on the horizon.

Mister Woodhouse's Notes

Jessie—Zeppelin—23 keys
Strategy: She's definitely hawking the keys for silver. I also suspect she stole Ben's keys off him while the others were waiting for Rupert and Camilla

Benjamin—Zeppelin—0 keys
Strategy: Keeping quiet

Camilla—Zeppelin—0 keys
Strategy: Something has changed in her.

Rupert—Zeppelin—0 keys
Strategy: Cuddling with Camilla

Maple—Zeppelin—2 keys
Strategy: Controlling her fighting impulses

Zenith—Zeppelin—23 keys
Strategy: Sitting suspiciously close to Jessie

Vault-Destroyed?

This twisted game is finally over, at least for me.

Now, my daughter and I can build a new life for ourselves in a place without automatons or vaults or any more of these wretched keys.

Perhaps these competitors have finally learned what I concluded long ago: chasing money often leads to far more trouble than it's worth.

Epilogue

Zenith, the Assassin

Six Months Later

I CAST A GLANCE behind me into the shadows of the alley, then look back down at my timepiece, my mother's initials snagging my gaze for the briefest instant. The air is thick in the narrow gap between the towering buildings where I've hidden myself, but I've spent time in tighter spaces. The vibrant city life buzzes past, oblivious as usual.

Since Arden's death, I've had to keep my eyes in all directions. Despite how nicely I packaged the details and how much Ben has been suffering through his imprisonment, Mr. Bentley will never forgive my failure. There had been no pot of gold at the end of the event, and the closest thing to a rainbow had been the fireworks as Sky Manor had exploded into flames behind our escaping zeppelin.

Images from our harrowing escape race through my mind. Camilla clinging to Rupert. Woodhouse's eyes, alive with joy while reuniting with his daughter. Jessie and Maple's soot-and-tear-stained cheeks. Ben's rage. Even in that moment, I'd only been able to catch these things in snatches, knowing I'd have to hit the ground running to avoid punishment from my enraged employer. I'd crushed our communication device, but I knew I'd be hard-pressed to find other employment in the area as long as Mr. Bentley maintained power.

My vision focuses on my current quarry. These past six months, I've been tasked with a very different type of job than my usual. With Ben's imprisonment and consequent removal from his grandfather's will, Rupert found himself in possession of an inheritance I must admit he deserves. He's surprised me with his shrewd head for business and commitment to ensuring the other contestants are properly cared for.

He's also hired me to keep an eye on Camilla. As much as I'd like to catch her slipping poisons into her pocket to sell at absurd prices in back alleys, she seems to have committed herself to her work at the apothecary, and has even forgone the need for the newest dresses in order to help care for her family.

As she swishes through the apothecary door, her gown is stylish but not frivolous. I believe I will soon be able to assure Rupert that the love she continues to proclaim for him is genuine. Thus far, he has chosen not to inform her of the substantial fortune he has come into, instead visiting her in the same rumpled suit he wore at Sky Manor.

Leaning back into the shadows, I wander away from the busy street. I pick up my pace, passing from the polite areas of town into the outskirts. Despite my focus on staying unnoticed in the shadows, my thoughts flicker to the letter I received the week before from Ben, of all people. He'd rambled on about an old prisoner turned chaplain who'd convicted him of his evil ways. I talked it over with Jessie when I first got it, and we remain skeptical to say the least. He did confess that he'd accepted a contract from Arden to kill Mr. Bentley in exchange for a sizable sum. When he overheard Arden talking to Jessie and expressing his desire to be a better man in the future, he feared that the contract would go by the wayside, taking the large payout with it. This worry, he claimed, drove him over the edge and led him to push Arden to his doom.

My attention shifts to the orphan home as I approach it. Rupert has been having me secretly deposit money into the home's account, and Jessie has worked wonders with the place. It's amazing what a fresh coat of paint and a smattering of potted plants can do to brighten things up in this dismal part of the city, not to mention the way the children have all been shined up with new clothes, better food, and the addition of a tutor to assist in their education. While I've kept the source of the money a secret, I have not been quite as clandestine with my own intentions.

I stop some distance away, watching Jessie sweep the front steps as a pair of boys wrestle on the sidewalk. When one of them lets out a grunt of pain, she taps the broom on the metal railing of the porch, and they break apart to resume their game of marbles.

"There's no need to hide in the shadows, Zenith." Jessie's bright eyes sparkle as she glances my way. She still moves with the grace of a thief, but thankfully, she no longer has to rely on her criminal skills to provide for the children, even without Mr. Bentley acknowledging her position as his daughter.

I step into the sun and give her a half-smile, handing her a somewhat crumpled paper bag. "Maple sends her best." I haven't quite gotten accustomed to grinning, but Jessie's expression of joy has a strange impact on my composure.

She opens the bag and inhales deeply. "Peach scones! These things are divine. Please tell me you've tried one already. I'll share if you haven't, but . . ."

"These are just for you," I assure her with a wink. "She wouldn't let me leave without trying her newest creation: 'I Ardently Admire You' cinnamon rolls."

A look passes over Jessie's face, a cross between sadness and a curious pride. "I never got the chance to know Arden well, but seeing Maple honor my brother like this . . ." She sighs, clearly moved by the mixture of emotions she hasn't figured out how to deal with yet. She takes a bite of her pastry, pushing the cloud away from her features. "Do you have time to come in today?"

I hate to douse the hope in her eyes, but I promised Rupert a full report this afternoon. The diamond ring he's been carrying around for the past six months is about to burn a hole in his pocket if I don't give him the go ahead to propose to Camilla soon.

"Maybe next time." My eyes flick back down the alley. The last thing I want to do is spend too much time in the daylight. I've a feeling Mr. Bentley is keeping eyes on Jessie, too, just in case she tries to push the issue of her parentage.

"Take care of yourself, Zenith." Her touch is feather-light on my arm before she turns back to the orphan home.

The shadows swallow me. I maneuver through the back roads toward the office Rupert has rented, eager to give him the news.

Just as I reach his building, something flutters through the air. I catch it on instinct but nearly drop it when I realize what it is. A deep green envelope, embossed with a golden key.

Impossible. The manor was destroyed. We all saw it explode into fragments too small to be pieced back together.

Fingers trembling, I slit the envelope with my favorite dagger, then pull out a single sheet of paper.

You Are Invited

No one won though one did die

Riches untouched await in the sky

The stolen keys must be returned

Until the treasure is rightly earned

Enemies turned friends must reunite

Will friendships last, or devolve in the fight?

Return for the search, keep your weapons drawn

The Game is not over, Sky Manor not gone

The truth remains, unlock treasures within

For one must die, and **One Must Win**

Acknowledgments

Thank you to all our families for your love and support during this project and many others. Your ongoing support allows us to do what we do.

Thank you to the Christian Mommy Writers. These six authors found each other and this book exists thanks to the wonderful, supportive CMW community. Thank you for cheering us on, and for being an ongoing encouragement and resource to all of us. We hope you enjoyed the eccentric Mr. Woodhouse, and Maple's delicious Screaming Peach scones.

Thank you to our beta readers: Tiffany Goldman, Dani Renee, and Megan Parmerter. Your encouragement and feedback gave us the fresh perspective we needed to make this story stronger and more cohesive!

Thank you to Selina De Luca for generously lending your proofreading skills to this book. Thanks to you, our words now shine all the more.

We give thanks to God for granting us our gifts and talents and allowing us to work together on this project. May our words bring Him glory!

Finally, a special thanks to all our advanced readers. We appreciate your enthusiasm for *One Must Die*. Advanced reader names will be listed below:

Stephany Araujo, Laina Porter, Crystal Roberts, Kelly Tenuta, Storm Shultz, Elise Haroldson, Stephanie Daniels, IyanuOluwa Olorode, Abigail Langton, Becky Briggs, Natalie Ehinger, Carla Harding, Ridaa Sultan, Melanie Chapman, Rosina Campbell, Deborah Ortega, Amaya Joy Anderson, Jennifer Macaulay, Erin Dydek, Serret Samson, Abby Diehl, Kim Rayburn, Megan Barnes, Sara Rosevear, Megan McLellan, Karla Holdier, Melissa Rampton, Summer, Iris Maya, Mel Seeley, Courtney Denelsbeck, Lyss Lance, Kathleen Grymes, Sabrina Swartzentruber, Isabelle Martin, Kathy Crowder, Faithful Aki, Linda Badcock, Chloe Moody, Ma. Joanne A. Aguilera, Bethany Aich, Sasha, Ashlea Adams, Cynthia Ann Topp, Stephany Araujo, Kailey Bechtel, Katelin Ross, Jessie Clark, Lizzie Porter, Heather Davidson, D. T. Powell, Sara Rosevear, Jennifer Macaulay, Emma Hecker, Nathan Trimble, Linda Badcock, Rachel Mason, Megan Barnes, Kayt Southworth, Hope Capps, Connie Schreiner, Amanda Keller.

About the Author

Candice Pedraza Yamnitz fell in love with *The Lord of the Rings* and *Pride and Prejudice* in high school and hasn't stopped reading since. She taught in a dual-language elementary classroom for years until she decided to stay at home, teaching a crew of imaginative children. In between reading lessons and converting cardboard boxes into pirate ships, she writes YA novels with a Latin twist. She lives in her native Chicagoland. Visit her at candiceyamnitz.com and find her on Instagram and TikTok at @candiceyamnitz.

Also By Candice...

UNBETROTHED

RUTHLESS

DESSI AND KY GO POOF

DEAR MOUSE PRINCESS

About the Author

Hailing from the Midwest plains where clouds and imagination roam, Amber Lambda is a young adult author, homeschool mom, K-drama and manga enthusiast, and a life-long dreamer. Though Amber's ideas vary on the scale of whimsy and realism, her writer's heart belongs to stories that are appropriate for the YA audience and filled with a blend of relatable characters, sweet romance, and relevant themes that will stay with the reader long after the last page.

Also By Amber...

HALOS

COMETS FADE WITH SUMMER

About the Author

Sarah Everest has been writing stories for as long as she has been able to form letters with a pencil. She has traveled the world, taking photos, gathering ideas and experiencing places and cultures that help to shape her creativity and landscapes. She currently lives in the Czech Republic with her husband, daughter, and their dog.

Also By Sarah...

DAWN OF THE DARKENING

THE DARKENING DRAGONS

PEAK DRAGON UPRISING

BOHEMIAN DRAGON AWAKENING

ONE WEEK IN NOVEMBER

VEILED IN FOG

About the Author

Claire Kohler is a historical romantasy author and neurodiversity advocate. She is also an editor and tutor. When she's not working, you'll find her chasing her two small children, binging Korean dramas, and leading Bible studies at her church. She and her husband live with their son and daughter in North Carolina.

Also By Claire...

THE ANGEL OF TORIN WOODS
THE SECRET OF DRULEA COTTAGE
THE HEART OF EVERTON INN
THE TREASURE OF RIGMORE HOUSE

About the Author

Lydia Mae has been writing about adventures, new worlds, and princesses since she could put words to paper. When she isn't writing, Lydia enjoys serving in her church, teaching, musical theater, and quality time with her husband and two precious children. You can find more about her writing at authorlydiamae.com

Also By Lydia...

TO BREAK A SILENCE: A LITTLE MERMAID
RETELLING

About the Author

Clean books with guaranteed happily ever afters.

C.C. Urie is a Michigan author who has a fierce love for autumn and Jesus. Her son is her greatest joy and the center of her world. She discovered a love for reading at a young age, and ever since she's wanted to share meaningful stories that stayed with people long after they closed the book. Her biggest goal in life is to share the stories God has shared with her.

Also By C.C. Urie...

THE DIVINE COURAGE TRILOGY

Anthologies

TALES FROM THE BACKCOUNTRY

TWISTED GRIMMS

Preview of Zenith's Story

by Sarah Everest, One Must Die Spin-off Book Coming 2025

"Hush now, my child." A shaking hand passed over my forehead, leaving a sticky trail swirling up into my hair that smelled of iron and salt. Strong hands lifted me from my bed, and I wrapped my small arms around my mother's neck, breathing in the familiar aroma of her skin, letting the earthiness of her sweat drown out the stench of death that clung to her fingers.

"Where are we going?" My voice quivered in the warm night air. It was not the first time she had lifted me from my dreams and carried me away, though any memories of other homes were only shadowy figures in my mind.

She gave no response, save for the ticking of her heart and the rush of her hair cascading around my head as we vanished into the night.

I AWOKE ON A rough, straw-stuffed pallet. Through heavy eyes, I watched sparks leap from my mother's blades as she struck them against her sharpening stone. The clang and slick, metallic slide hummed through the room.

"Go back to sleep, Zenith." Without once glancing in my direction, she silenced my questions. I knew better than to speak after such a command. I wiggled deeper beneath the blanket, willing myself back to sleep, but was greeted only by fear behind my darkened eyelids.

I had left the little black dog on my pillow, the one precious thing I had carried with me for as long as my memories stretched into the past. We would not go back, and two desires warred within my chest as I thought of my furry companion: the hope that my only toy would bring joy to another, and the wish that no one else would ever find it, leaving me as the only one who would ever love it.

The room stilled, and my mother rose, coming to stand over me.

"You can stop pretending to be asleep." She squatted down, and I cracked my eyes open, studying the tattoos that fluttered over her shoulders and crept up the edges of her neck. I only knew of death as something that hunched in the shadows, its greedy fingers grasping for anyone unlucky enough to be written on the list it carried, the list it frequently passed to my mother and her knives. But I was wary of the dark ink sparkling against her pale skin. It haunted my dreams if I thought on it too much.

"Happy birthday." Her words took me as much by surprise as the bundle she pressed into my palm. I sat up, a rush of longing chasing away the cloudy bits of sleep from my mind. For the briefest moment, I wondered if she had picked up my scrappy dog after all, but the bundle had far too much weight to be my treasured toy.

"Open it," she urged, settling onto the lumpy mattress.

My fingers trembled in anticipation as I unwound the cord securing the bit of cloth. My breath caught in my throat as the early morning light shone on cold metal. A thin blade with a handle the perfect size to rest comfortably in my hand glinted up at me.

"I was given my first dagger on my fifth birthday." She stroked my dark hair as her eyes focused on something I couldn't see. I waited for her to continue, but there were no more words to her story. Like usual.

I remained frozen until her hand on my head grew heavy. I wanted to say something, but thank you felt too small in the face of such a momentous gift.

A rooster crowed somewhere in the distance. It was enough to tell me we were no longer in the city, and it broke her from her trance. Her hand stilled on my hair, and she looked back to my eyes. "Today will be your first lesson in throwing blades. But not with this one." She shook her head and folded the fabric back around my present. "We will start with wooden stakes until you are steady enough not to chip the blade."

I followed her from the darkness into the dim light of the early morning, trying to figure out where we might be. Ravens watched us as we walked into a circle of trees. I wanted to reach for my mother's fingers when one of them mimicked a baby crying, but she would only brush my hand away. Instead, I reached up to push my hair from my eyes and felt something crusted on my forehead. I pulled my fingers back and stared at the dark reddish-brown flakes clinging to them.

We stopped in the middle of the clearing. Mother pointed to a circle carved into the bark of the largest tree. "That is your target." She marched me to the tree and spun me around so the trunk pressed against my back. Then she took five long paces and beckoned me to join her. "You will throw until every hit is on the mark."

A dagger sang from its sheath as she whipped it into the air and hurled it at the target. The largest of the ravens took flight with an angry shriek and considerable flapping. The blade sank deep into the tree's flesh with a satisfying thwack. But Mother didn't even watch long enough to see it make contact. She was already handing me the stake, positioning it in my hand to throw.

My first attempts were haphazard at best, though only one slapped the tree on the flat side and fell to the ground. A few errant throws made several more of the ravens flutter after their supposed leader. I kept at it, ignoring the squalling birds. The stakes were sharpened enough to stick when I threw them straight. After a handful of minutes, I hit the target for the first time, and by the end of half an hour, every throw was a strike.

Mother's only reaction was a mild snort of approval, followed by a directive to take a long stride backward and begin again.

My hands ached at the end of the day, but still they clung to the dagger. Mother had finally decided to let me throw it by midday, and as the sky darkened, I hit the target with a loud thud. I chanced a look at her, but she wasn't watching me anymore. Instead, she flipped her time piece through her fingers, so fast it made my head spin. I couldn't remember the last time we had taken a break to drink, and we had eaten nothing all day. My legs wobbled, and she spun miraculously, her arms catching me a second before I struck the ground.

"Perhaps that's enough for today." Her laughter sent the last of the ravens soaring with angry cries. "You have done well, Zenith."

The praise of my mother soaked through my skin, a warmth that drove away the coldness of the coming night. She released her grip on me, and I sighed, relieved that my balance continued to hold steady. With a flick of her wrist, the pocket watch she'd been spinning sailed into the air, and she caught it in the small leather pouch strapped to her arm over the tattoo of a hangman's tree.

COMING 2025